PRAISE FOR CHRIS D.'s

"Imagine THELMA & LOUISE, Jim Thompson and punk rock folded together in a high-speed blender and you've got VOLCANO GIRLS. Chris D. imbues noir *with a vibe that rocks hard."*

– Alan K. Rode, author of
CHARLES MCGRAW, FILM NOIR TOUGH GUY and
MICHAEL CURTIZ, A MAN FOR ALL MOVIES

"The sound of a pick-axe, the smell of the half-drunk bourbon, the feel of the shock-absorberless truck, the sight of a head evaporating in an aerosol shower of blood – sensurround noir, *by a writer who doesn't hold back."*

– Sylvie Simmons, author of
the short story collection, TOO WEIRD FOR ZIGGY
and I'M YOUR MAN: THE LIFE OF LEONARD COHEN

PRAISE FOR CHRIS D.'s NOVEL MOTHER'S WORRY

"MOTHER'S WORRY swaps midnight for high noon; Chris D. burns down the speakeasy and pool hall and drags the roman noir *across the desert dirt beneath an unforgiving sun. This is my kind of crime novel."*

– Craig Clevenger, author of
the novels THE CONTORTIONIST'S HANDBOOK
and DERMAPHORIA

"Next time you're set on stealing some cash and a car and bombing your blood-soaked way across Mexico in a barrage of bullets, bitches and badasses – just read MOTHER'S WORRY instead. You'll get the same adrenaline rush, minus the jail time."

– Eddie Muller, author of
DARK CITY DAMES,
DARK CITY: THE LOST WORLD OF FILM NOIR,
and the novels THE DISTANCE and SHADOW BOXER

PRAISE FOR CHRIS D.'s NOVEL SHALLOW WATER

"One sinister serpent of a story, an old Republic Pictures western serial scripted by James M. Cain and reimagined by Sam Peckinpah. I loved it. Dive in and wallow in SHALLOW WATER"

– Eddie Muller

WHAT WRITERS HAD TO SAY ABOUT CHRIS D.'S ANTHOLOGY
A MINUTE TO PRAY, A SECOND TO DIE

"Reading Chris D.'s blood-on-the-page prose is like running naked, screaming with terror and desire, through the fetid back alleys of American pulp culture. You're seduced, fucked over, doused with whiskey, set on fire, dragged by the getaway car, nailed by the hail from a 30.06 and still, still – you can't stop reading."

– Eddie Muller, author of
the novels, THE DISTANCE and SHADOW BOXER

"...he continues a tradition in writing that is all but lost; authors who use their powers of imagination and creativity rather than simply recounting or inventing a memoir. Like the outsider artists that Chris D. champions, he writes for the future, for art, to someday be truly discovered for the great talent he is."

– John Doe, singer/songwriter
of X and THE KNITTERS

"Chris D. presents...such an immense encapsulation of his life's work that it reads as literary autopsy of a man not yet dead but of one who has died a thousand times and somehow miraculously between crucifixions used pen as shovel to prevent himself from being buried alive."

– Lydia Lunch, musician and author of
PARADOXIA and WILL WORK FOR DRUGS

"To my mind, the lyrics he wrote...are as blinding a display of raw, universe-gobbling intelligence as have ever been penned...The sources from which Chris drew his inspiration are a classic pop cultural blend – exploitation films of all stripes, pulp fiction, French decadent poets, hot rod gangs, mystical Catholicism, underground biker comix, beatnik booze into the hippie acid continuum, and on and on and on. This is a mix that has gained great subterranean currency over the past few decades, but when Chris was churning through these waters, they were as yet uncharted. His written work (along with that of fellow travelers such as Exene Cervenka, Dave Alvin, John Doe and Claude 'Kickboy' Bessy) created a new, totally crazed hipster aesthetic that rejected punk orthodoxy in favor of something much more magnificent and inclusive."

– Byron Coley, writer for WIRE Magazine,
author of C'EST LA GUERRE:
EARLY WRITINGS 1978-1983

TIGHTROPE
ON
FIRE

ALSO BY CHRIS D.

Double Snake Bourbon

A Minute to Pray, A Second to Die

No Evil Star

Dragon Wheel Splendor and Other Love Stories of Violence and Dread

Shallow Water

Volcano Girls

NON-FICTION

Outlaw Masters of Japanese Film

Gun and Sword: An Encyclopedia of Japanese Gangster Films, 1955–1980

TIGHTROPE ON FIRE

BY

CHRIS D.

A POISON FANG BOOK

If you enjoy this book, tell someone about it

A Poison Fang Book

Original screenplay © 2001 by Chris Desjardins, pka Chris D.

Novel © 2013 by Chris Desjardins, pka Chris D.

Front and back cover designs by C. D.

ISBN: 0615819834

First Poison Fang Edition, October 2013

Printed in the United States

10 9 8 7 6 5 4 3 2 1

For Craig O., *thanks...*

PROLOGUE

ARTICLE: *FROM THE SWEET HOME POST, JANUARY 28, 1988*

LOCAL PHILANTHROPIST
COMMITTED TO ASYLUM

Betty Richman, wife of noted millionaire entrepreneur Jack 'Satch' Richman and a beloved philanthropist who contributed to charities in Sweet Home and Desert Hot Springs has apparently suffered a nervous breakdown after several undisclosed personal health setbacks. She was taken to the Samuel Thurgood Memorial Sanitarium in Palm Springs and is currently being evaluated by her doctor and sanitarium staff members. Her husband, Mr. Richman was not available for comment. His secretary, Marilyn Packard, reported he is inconsolable and his prime concern at the moment is the welfare of his young twin daughters, Valerie and Vanessa.

ARTICLE: *FROM THE PALM SPRINGS SENTINEL, JUNE 10, 1988*

SHERIFF'S DETECTIVE AND SON
DIE IN MYSTERY FIRE

Richard Manning, 31, a homicide detective in the County Sheriff's Office in Sweet Home, and his son Joseph, 6, succumbed to the effects of burns and smoke inhalation from a devastating fire that left their house on the outskirts of Sweet Home all but destroyed. Sweet Home Fire Department personnel are mystified by the cause of the blaze and have not ruled out arson as a possible cause. The two deceased are survived by wife and mother, Francine, also an officer with the Sweet Home Sheriffs, who was on duty and not at home at the time of the conflagration. Manning was thrust into an unwelcome spotlight in early 1986 when he uncovered evidence exonerating millionaire businessman Jack Richman of murder charges in the shooting death of real estate developer Clancy Hepburn. At the time, controversy swirled around the case due to the blood relation of Manning's wife, Francine, to Richman, her uncle.

1

Frankie Powers' pupils convulsed in r.e.m. beneath her bruised eyelids. Somewhere in the ether, poised between heaven and hell where Satan monitored her vital signs and gave a pitiless shrug over the two mean bulletholes in her chest, Frankie heard her own voice from a few days previous, "I guess you must enjoy going from the frying pan into the fire."

Blue flames reared up around her, turning bright orange, then yellow, then finally a blinding white light, destroying her happy suburban home so many years before.

Outside in the town square, the summer California sun beat down relentlessly on the nearly deserted main street and county courthouse. Deputy Seymour Knox perched atop the hood of his patrol car, reading the newspaper. 72 pt. type read: DETECTIVE POWERS SENTENCED TODAY. Suddenly the headline contorted as Knox crumpled the paper. He threw it in the nearby trash can, spit in the gutter, then

turned to face the courthouse. There was the low rumble of
a crowd approaching.

A teeming pack of media, legal personnel, sheriff's
deputies and townspeople exploded out of the courthouse
doors into the sunlight.

Frankie Powers, a disheveled woman in her mid-
thirties, weary and manacled, was buffeted towards the
street by a sea of people. Her left hand was heavily
bandaged. Reporters yelled at her and at her deputy escorts,
trying to edge their way close enough to her to get a
comment or good camera angle.

Cecilia, a blonde, dreadlocked teenage crackhead
with a crazy look in her eyes, emerged from the alley across
the plaza. She crossed the street, edging her way through
the crowd and up to the oblivious Frankie, drawing a Glock
from the waistband of her low slung bellbottom jeans.

Young, dark haired Vanessa Richman was wallking
slightly behind Frankie, Sheriff Manny Torres and his
deputies, but she was the first to spot Cecilia and realize
the danger. She tried to rush ahead of Frankie, her hands
outstretched.

"No, Ceci, don't!"

Cecilia fired almost point blank into Frankie's chest.
There was an immediate welling up of screams and shouts,
the already agitated throng becoming a panicking swarm.
Sheriff Torres and his deputies all grabbed Cecilia and
wrestled the gun away. For a few seconds, Frankie was held
upright by the crowd. There was a strange look of serenity
on her makeup-free features. She crumpled to the asphalt in
what seemed like slow motion.

Vanessa stood isolated, paralyzed with disbelief,
looking down at Frankie as the deputies tried to keep
control of the crowd.

A little boy with a balloon tentatively approached
Frankie from out of the crisscross chaos of running people
and gazed down at her. His mother fluttered to him, one

hand to her own mouth and the other over the boy's eyes as she nudged him quickly away.

Frankie smiled as she watched the balloon get knocked from the boy's grasp and drift upwards into the azure sky.

A pair of pupils convulsed in r.e.m. beneath Frankie's bruised eyelids. She was unconscious in her hospital bed.

Frankie watched the handheld video of herself, her late husband Rick Manning and late son Joey for the umpteenth time – all enjoying a Saturday afternoon together. Frankie, sunglasses on and a cigarette dangling from her smiling mouth, pushed steaks around on a barbecue with a metal spatula. Rick came up from behind, hugged her around her waist and kissed her on her ear. Laughing, she took the cigarette from her mouth and turned to playfully push his face away. Rick headed towards the camera, took it and moved off-screen so Frankie's dad, Nick Powers, came into view. There was an eerie cry of echoey voices on the sound-track, as if the action was happening a long ways away. Frankie stood waving with son Joey in her arms in the driveway of a tract house in the desert. Frankie's dad Nick kissed the boy and her, then moved off jauntily to his car.

There was a jagged lightning bolt across the desert's night sky, and a rattlesnake struck out at her face.

Frankie's pupils convulsed in r.e.m. beneath her bruised eyelids. She was unconscious in her hospital bed, on life support. Vanessa stood in the doorway with Sheriff Torres. Vanessa moved towards the bed. Torres reached out to hold her arm, but she petulantly yanked herself away. She sank to her knees by Frankie's face. Tears ran down her own cheeks.

"Don't die, Frankie. Please don't die."

It was late morning under a blazing sun outside a 1950s vintage apartment house.

Frankie headed up a short stairway, knocked perfunctorily, then barged right in. Her father, Nick Powers, was wheelchair-bound, looking out his enormous picture window at the vast empty expanse of dried out land. Frankie surveyed the clutter without removing her sunglasses.

"Dad, look at this place. You haven't had that cleaning woman come in, have you?"

Nick had a petulant expression on his face and wouldn't look at her.

"I gave you money to get a maid in here, someone to organize and tidy up this mess."

Nick turned his wheelchair around to face her. "I wouldn't use that money to wipe –" He literally bit his tongue.

Frankie made a face. "What did you do with it, then?"

Nick pointed at the microwave sitting on the bar counter between the living room and kitchen. Frankie opened it, and a pile of cash fell out.

"I know where you got that dough. It's goddamn dirty money, Frankie. From your son-of-a-bitch Uncle Jack or one of his cronies."

Frankie didn't even pick up the cash, just slumped her butt against the counter, grabbed the half-full bottle of bourbon there and poured herself half a glass. She extended the bottle to Nick.

He shook his head, "Nah. Shit, that stuff barely even makes a dent in me anymore."

Frankie gave a cynical laugh, "Gee, Dad, maybe you should get yourself to one of those AA meetings."

"Everything's a joke to you, Frankie. Ever since your mother died and they promoted you to detective."

"As if things were any different then." Distracted,

Frankie picked up a framed photo from a shelf. "You mean since Rick and Joey died, don't you?"

Nick looked down at his lap. "This town's ruined you, Frankie."

She handed the photo to Nick. In it, she stood clad in blue jeans, T-shirt and sunglasses with her husband Rick and their son Joey between them. They were all smiling. "This town isn't what ruined me, Dad."

Nick was embarrassed and turned to look out the picture window again.

Frankie took back the photo, reverently replaced it and suddenly got angry.

"Stop going on like there were some golden, hallowed good ole days because there weren't. Rick and I had our problems, even back then."

"Living in this town and seeing what her no good brother, your Uncle Jack, was doing to it, killed your mother. It helped to kill Rick and Joey."

"You're imagining things —"

"Am I? It's gonna kill me. And kill you, too."

"Dad —"

"You know Jack's not just running pot in from Mexico. He's bringing in heroin and coke. And those girls he's recruiting for the Nevada whorehouses are underage."

"No, they're not." Frankie felt a familiar twinge of guilt and became defensive, "And they know what the fuck they're doing."

"You'll see."

"Dad, I don't have time for a lecture. And I'm not in the mood for hearing about your beef with the department. About how they whitewashed the shooting that put you in that goddamn wheelchair."

Nick just looked at her, hurt in his tough old eyes. Frankie realized that she had gone too far.

"I'm sorry, Dad. I didn't mean that."

"Yeah, you did. It's okay, baby. Maybe I had it

coming."

He paused. There was an uneasy silence as Frankie
drained her glass.

"You're walking around blind in a closet full of
alligators. You better watch out 'cause one is going to bite
you in the ass."

Frankie grimaced and shook her head. She picked
up the cash from the floor, stuffed it back in the microwave
and started to leave.

"Frankie –"

She turned, took off her sunglasses and used her
untucked shirttails to wipe them.

"– there's something weird going on with your
cousins, Jack's twins Vanessa and Valerie."

"Those two spoiled brat bimbos. So what else is
new."

"Stop being a smartass, Frankie. I'm not kidding.
That boy Jimmy who used to help out after I got shot –
Valerie's sweetheart, I think – he called me and he's
worried."

Frankie was incredulous, "Jimmy Chavez? That kid
is in hot water ninety percent of the time himself. You
cannot be serious."

"That's just it. He's no angel. And if he's worried,
he probably has good reason to be. He said Jack's trying to
make them do things.

"Do things?"

"Yeah."

Frankie shook her head, "What things?"

"You goddamn well know. Sex things. Happy now
that I said it? Whenever and whatever it is goes down, I
won't say I told you so."

She waved her hands like she'd had enough, kissed
him on the forehead as she passed by. Replacing her sunglasses, she slammed the screen door open and closed as
she split.

Nick looked after her, his hardened expression going suddenly wistful.

Outside, Frankie jumped into her car and angrily slammed the door. When she took off her sunglasses, tears poured soundlessly down her cheeks. She sank her head against the steering wheel.

A jagged lightning bolt cut across the desert's night sky.

Frankie's tract home was in full blaze. A fire engine was pulled into the driveway. Frankie screeched to a halt behind it and leapt out. She made for the house, but a fireman and Deputy Knox caught her from either side. She could not believe her eyes. There was an expression of shock and horror on her face. She turned from one to the other.

"Where's Rick and Joey!"

The fireman stared down at the ground, unable to look at her. Knox gazed grimly at the house. Frankie went wild.

"Where's my husband and son? Goddamn it! Where-the-fuck are they!"

She yanked free, and Knox barely caught her around one wrist. She tried to hit him in the face to free herself, but he blocked her hand, then slapped her.

"It's no use, Frankie. They're gone."

She stared at him, then around at the house, her mouth moving but unable to speak. She sank to her knees on the wet asphalt, sobbing, then let out a piercing scream.

2

Vanessa, her sister Valerie and their pal Cecilia walked hurriedly across the deserted street behind and into the shell of the boarded-up church. The bell tower, which was four blocks from the center of the microscopic town, had just struck high noon.

Inside, 19-year-old Jimmy Chavez sat atop the ruined altar in shafts of dustmoted sunlight. He was in the process of opening a bottle of Mexican beer when the girls showed up. He tossed each of them a bottle. "Hey, you get the weed?"

Vanessa answered, "Just barely. That fucking weasel Jay at the club was hemming and hawing about having to dip into his personal stash."

Valerie pulled a baggie of pot from her tight low slung jeans and quickly began rolling a joint next to Jimmy. "But Vanessa batted her eyelashes and promised Jay she'd go out with him." She leaned over as she rolled the reefer, giving Jimmy a wet open-mouthed kiss.

Cecilia put in her two cents, "Only thing is he'll never follow through because he's scared shitless of their old man."

Jimmy lit the joint as Valerie planted it between his lips. "Could also have something to do with Jack being his boss."

They passed the joint around, but when it got to Cecilia, she was too busy sucking on a crack pipe.

Vanessa was disgusted. "Shit. Ceci's broken out the rock. That's my cue to head back to school."

Jimmy was not happy, "Goddamn it, Cecilia –"

"Don't call me that. Call me Ceci!"

"Whatever. I wish you wouldn't smoke that shit in here. It stinks."

"It doesn't stink any worse than pot. And it's no worse for you neither."

Valerie contradicted her, "Oh, man, you didn't see those two girls who came through here last year. You didn't have to hang out with them. They lasted at the club one week before Jay had to get rid of them they were so fucked up behind that stuff."

"Fuck you guys!"

She jammed her pipe in her pocket and left in a huff.

Outside the church, she walked along the weed-choked, uneven sidewalk with the broiling ball of fire blazing down. Slowly a new black Buick pulled up to keep pace with her. A smile grew on her confused face as the mirrored automatic window rolled down.

Cal Nero was one of crime boss Jack Richman's prime henchmen. He was a slick, oily, good-looking monster with a perpetual venal grin plastered on his cruel features. He waved to her from the driver's seat.

"Hey, pretty girl, everything copacetic?"

He made the car keep up with her, and she blushed,

"What's that mean?"

He laughed. "Everything okay?"

She blushed again, embarrassed, "Yeah –"

"You need a lift anywhere?"

She stopped as the car stopped, nodded, then climbed in as he threw open the door. She became nervous as he broadened his sick grin.

"How you holding out with the rock there, baby?"

"I can always use as much as I can get".

"I heard that." He patted the empty space on the seat next to him. Cecilia slowly laid her head down on his upper thigh as he continued to drive. He let one hand trail to her face, gently petting her and smoothing her hair. She closed her eyes, hungry for and relishing the horrifically-motivated affection.

3

The law enforcement for the town was centered in the only
occupied buildings on the desolate main drag. A sign with
paint peeling read: SWEET HOME COUNTY SHERIFF.
Sunglasses-wearing Frankie stared between the slats of
the venetian blinds on the window behind Sheriff Manny
Torres' cluttered desk. He finished up his phone
conversation.

"Right, right. I understand...No, she's standing here
in my office right now...I'll tell her. You bet, Jerry."

He hung up the receiver, a look of consternation
spreading slowly across his worn and corpulent features.

He looked over at Frankie who was pre-occupied as
usual.

"That was our beloved mayor, Jerry Axelrod.
Wanted me to give you his regards. Christ, he's worse than
you, Frankie. Trying to get me to ease up on his 'pal' Jack
Richman. God-fearing, taxpaying, sweet-smelling Jack

Richman.

"A pillar of the community," Frankie added.

Torres shook his head and looked back down at his desk

"I can't figure you out, Frankie. Jack's behind alot more in this county than just minor vice. I'm pretty sure you know it."

"I don't know any such goddamn thing, Manny. So shut the fuck up."

"Touched a sore spot, hunh? Got a burr under the saddle."

She stared back out the window. Torres studied her ruefully.

"Spare me your stupid cowboy metaphors, Manny."

"So you don't know what's really going on in this town right under your nose? You're not a moron. And I used to think you had a conscience."

"I've got work to do. Anything else?"

"Yes, I've brought in a fellow to help you. What with the drugs and prostitution going up and up and those illegal guns seized last week, we need more than one detective. He's transferred here from Bakersfield. A good guy named Vince Farrell."

"Swell."

Torres looked sadly back down at his desk blotter. "Get the hell out of here."

Jack Richman's El Dorado sat at the top of the spiraling uphill driveway of his ranch house. Both back doors were open and someone could be heard singing *"Surrey With The Fringe on Top"*. Two legs protruded from the passenger side door. Burly, sixtyish Jack was cleaning the upholstery in the back seat, wiping copious bloodstains away with rags and continuing to hum to himself.

Jack Richman thought of himself as a ladies man,

and he had several Hollywood stars he would constantly reference for his self-image as lookalike role models: Ben Gazzara, poised somewhere between the sensitive doomed macho adventurer of his early career TV series *Run for Your Life* and his later lust-fueled, senior citizen mob boss Jackie Treehorn in the movie *The Big Lebowski.* Jack also idolized Raymond Burr in his pre-Perry Mason days, when he more often than not played sadistic, barrel-chested heavies in a succession of films noir.

Cal Nero and Marilyn Richman, Jack's tall demonic wife in her mid-fifties, approached the El Dorado.

Marilyn's voice was sing-songy, "Jaaackk. Oh, *Jaa-a-ckkk —*"

He poked his head out, annoyed at the interruption of his contented, egocentric reverie.

"What?"

Cal chimed in, "Why don't you let Ceci do that? She should do something to earn all that rock she keeps burning."

"You mean smoking your pole isn't enough, Cal?" He wrung out the rags in the bucket beside the car. "Nah, I like to do this. Helps me keep my finger on the pulse. Man, who would've ever thought that double-crossing, gun-dealing towel head had so much blood in him." Something occurred to him, " Hey, Marilyn, isn't it time for you to pick Vanessa up from school?"

Marilyn gave him a dirty look, took one last drag on her cigarette, stamped it out, then jumped into her Mustang. It roared to life, and she spun past the El Dorado down the hill.

4

Frankie stalked out of the Sheriff's building, got into
her car and lit up a smoke. She was desperately trying
to unwind. Something caught her attention, and she turned
to watch Sheriff Torres and the new plainclothes
detective, good-looking, fair-haired Vince Farrell head
down the block. They climbed into Torres' patrol car and
drove off.

Torres and Farrell pulled up across the street from Sweet
Home High School.
  "There's only about a hundred kids enrolled but
lately there's been a worrisome upswing in drug use.
Definitely out of proportion."
  A bell rang and almost immediately teenagers
started to spill out onto the grounds
  "Too be frank with you, Manny, I don't see how this
town is big enough to have even that many kids. Us just
cruising down the main drag, a person could think Sweet

Home's close to being a ghost town. Where're the jobs and
the homes?"

"These kids' families are spread out all over the
county. Some of their folks even commute into Nevada for
work at casinos. There's also a factory outside town that
employs a lot of people."

"Factory for what?"

"Maybe maintenance facility is a better description.
Repair of electronic poker games, slot machines for the
Nevada gaming industry. It's jointly owned by our mayor
Jerry Axelrod and Jack Richman. The two being in bed
together doesn't make investigating Richman any easier."

"You think Richman's behind the drug increase with
the kids?"

"Probably, but indirectly. It didn't get really that bad
until last year when he brought Cal Nero and Jay Hellinger
into work for him. Nero's his muscle and Hellinger runs
the strip club. I think they're siphoning off whatever Jack
won't miss. Jack's more concerned about moving stuff
in from Mexico to his Vegas connections. Sweet Home's
small potatoes."

Vanessa Richman suddenly appeared out of a throng
of kids. She sat on a low brick wall and immediately
immersed herself in a book.

"That feisty little thing is one of Jack Richman's
daughters. Name's Vanessa, one of the twins. They don't
look exactly alike but don't let that fool you. They were
born within fifteen minutes of each other."

"Where's the other one?"

"Dropped out of school. She's a little wilder.
Probably with her boyfriend, Jimmy Chavez, right about
now. He actually made it through and graduated a year and
a half ago. He's got a big mouth and smokes way too much
reefer. But I suppose he could be a helluva lot worse."

"So, the underage girls?"

"I don't have as clear a picture. Jack's not stupid enough to try to recruit any of the girls here for the Nevada houses he supplies. If the rumors are true, the underage girls are runaways from various places in central California. I've heard horror stories about Nero and Hellinger going out trawling through small towns, looking for cute little dumb dopeheads they can shanghai into service."

"Nothing to back it up?"

Torres shook his head as Marilyn Richman pulled to the curb not far from Vanessa.

Marilyn, a smoke hanging jauntily between her lips, swung open the door.

"Well, what're you waiting for?"

Vanessa gave Marilyn a cold stare.

Torres and Farrell watched as Marilyn tried to coax Vanessa off the wall outside the school. She was getting angry.

"Goddamn it, Vanessa. Lose the fucking attitude and just get in the car."

"That's Marilyn. Jack Richman's latest wife and Vanessa's stepmom."

Vanessa reluctantly acquiesced and climbed in.

"Christ, you'd think Richman's kids would have their own cars."

"No way. He's too much of a control freak. Word is he's pretty upset with Valerie right now for hanging out with the Chavez kid."

Marilyn put her foot on the gas and burned rubber.

"Goddamn bitch, Marilyn." He switched on the siren and took off after her. "She's knows better than that, driving hell bent for leather in a school zone." He sighed, "Jack committed their original mom to an institution about ten years ago. She was too decent. The more she found out about what Jack was really up to, the less she could handle it."

Marilyn stopped within a quarter of a mile.

Farrell trailed a good six paces behind Torres as he sidled up to Marilyn's side of the car. Torres finally stopped and just gazed down at the angry harridan.

"What is this, Manny? Are you crazy?"

"Zero to 60 in a 15 mile an hour school zone. With children present. Kids, in case you hadn't noticed. That's crazy."

"Kids? They're not kids. They're little adults. Little adults that should be thrashed within an inch of their lives at least once a week to remind them who is boss and keep them on their toes."

"Marilyn, do you really want to go through all this again?"

"Sure, Manny. Only because you do. You know this is nothing but a nuisance stop. A chickenshit beef. A $100 ticket. Try running me in, and I'll be out before the ink dries on your booking forms."

"Yeah, Marilyn. A nuisance call."

Vanessa was mortified and stared out her window into the surrounding desert and rundown buildings.

"So let's get it over with then. Can the goddamn lecture this time out. I've got an appointment to get my nails done. So, give me the goddamn ticket already, Manny, and stop trying to act like you've got a Federal case."

Torres wrote out the ticket, had her sign and tore her copy out of the pad.

"Thanks, Manny and fuck off." Once more, she slammed her foot on the accelerator, burned rubber and was gone in a cloud of dust.

"She is bad news."

"You better believe it." They sauntered back to the

cruiser. "A real bitch on wheels. Used to be a dominatrix in
Texas. If the sex slave traffic is really going on, like I think,
Marilyn's a big fucking part of it."

"And what about Jack's niece, Detective Powers?"

Torres became sad, "I wish I knew. I've known her
since she was little. She could be a real hellion in her own
right. But she used to be a sweetheart, too. Everything I
know about –" He paused, frustrated. "Her dad Nick used
to be on the force. Until he got shot a few years ago. We're
not sure exactly what went down there or who it was. Nick
and I don't exactly see eye-to-eye anymore. Thinks I'm
too soft on Richman!" Torres let out a deep breath. "When
Frankie's husband Rick, the detective I told you about,
when he and their son died, she went off the deep end.
I don't know if she's going to finally come up for air or
drown."

Coming in out of the desert sun, the bar was almost black
inside. Sunglasses-wearing Frankie was at the counter,
nursing a drink. Smiling Vince Farrell sat self-confidently
down next to her. Frankie glanced at him and spotted the
badge and gun clipped to the belt of his blue jeans.

"What're you so goddamn happy about?"

Farrell signaled to the bartender, "Give me a
Tecate," then turned his attention to Frankie, "I'm forty-two
years old, and I'm just grateful to still be sucking air.

"Yeah, I guess some of us take that for granted.
Even in our line of work."

"It's an easy thing to take for granted."

A soulful R&B ballad sung by a female singer
welled up on the jukebox.

"I love this song." He paused, "Did you put this
on?"

She nodded, "Why did you think I put it on?"

"Because nobody else in here looks like they have

any taste."

As if on cue, lumbering deputy Knox came out of the men's room and up to Frankie. He slapped her on the back.

"Hey, Powers! What's shakin' there, kiddo?"

She whispered under her breath, "Speak of the devil."

"You got a horoscope for me today?"

Frankie looked over at him then back at her drink. She pinched the bridge of her nose in mock concentration. "Yeah, yeah – I got a horoscope for you. Stay out of bottomless pits for the next month."

Knox guffawed and slapped Frankie on the back again, almost making her spill her drink. "Powers, you are a *genuwine* scream! Too much!" He looked at Farrell, "I can always depend on Frankie to make me laugh." He stumbled out of the bar, shaking his head with mirth.

Once again, there was an uneasy silence between Frankie and Farrell. He finally broke the ice, extending his hand.

"My name's Vince Farrell. I just transferred here from Bakersfield. Narcotics."

Frankie took off her sunglasses and looked him in the eye. She took his hand.

"Glad to meet you. I'm Frankie Powers. Manny told me someone was coming in from out of town to give me a hand. I've been pulling triple duty between homicide, narcotics and vice ever since I got promoted to detective nine years ago. What made you transfer here? Bakersfield too big for you?"

"Believe it or not. That was part of it, I guess. Even though it's not that big to begin with. It can get a bit rough on a Saturday night. And there's signs the biker gangs are upping meth production."

Frankie shook her head.

"What?"

"Nothing. I guess you must enjoy going from the frying pan into the fire."

"What do you mean? It's worse here?"

Frankie put her sunglasses back on. "You'll see."

At Frankie's house outside town, a pair of legs clad in blue jeans and cowboy boots protruded from under a vintage car with the hood open in the dirt driveway.

Vince Farrell pulled up in a patrol car. Clad in black jeans and a long sleeve white shirt, he tentatively moved towards the car. He stopped short, peering down at the feet and clearing his throat. "Excuse me, can you tell me where I can find Frankie Powers?"

The legs backpedaled and a grease-smeared Frankie in a tanktop slid from under the chassis.

"Christ, I must really be losing my touch." She flipped off her footwear. "I didn't think my legs looked like a boy's just because I had on jeans and boots. I guess I was wrong."

Vince was furiously blushing.

She stuck one foot up in the air and wriggled her painted toenails at him. "How's that, Farrell? Can you tell I'm a girl now?"

"Jesus, you're a real ballbuster, aren't you?"

She shook her head in frustration, then grabbed the half gone six-pack sitting near the curb. She pulled one off and threw it to him. He barely snagged it before it hit the ground.

"I know you dig Mexican beer."

They both took long swallows, and there was an uneasy silence.

"You don't have to worry about being mistaken for a boy, Frankie. You fill out a tanktop nicely."

"Well, I'm not filling it out for you."

She started to move back under the undercarriage. He shrugged, drained the beer, set it on top of her car and turned away. She poked her head out again from under the bumper.

"So, Farrell, what'd you come here for anyway."

He crouched down next to her. "I thought –"

"C'mon, c'mon don't be shy."

"I thought maybe we could go to the movies later."

"The only movie theater in town closed last October."

"But there's a –"

"– movie title up on the marquee on the place in town? It's been up for the last year. They just left it there ever since the doors shut for good. Jack Richman's turning it into a strip club. As if we needed another one."

"Richman's your uncle, isn't he?"

"Don't remind me."

"Well, I guess that's it."

"Jeez, you give up easy. You know we could go out to dinner instead. There's a nice place about two miles outside town. We've got to be done by six, though. I've a short shift going seven to midnight."

5

Farrell pulled his car into the parking lot of The Round Up Room, a place that looked as if it had been built in the fifties.

The lighting was low and atmospheric. Some mellow jazz that sounded like fifties Miles Davis played on the jukebox. Farrell and Frankie were silhouetted in a shaft of golden light as they made their way inside. Frankie was clad in a simple, but pretty house dress. There was only one other slightly older couple seated at the bar.

May, a hostess in her late forties, appeared.

"Drinks or dinner?"

"Both."

"Oh, hey, Frankie. I didn't recognize you for a minute. Gosh, how long has it been?"

"Four or five months ago. I was in here with Jack and his wife, Marilyn."

It was an unhappy memory for May. "Oh, yeah."

Marilyn had taken a drink off a tray before May had had time to set it down. The three of them – Frankie, Jack and Marilyn – were already soused and laughing uproariously. Marilyn had taken a sip, choked, then spit it out across the table as she ricocheted upwards and out of her seat, causing May to spill the other drinks on Jack. Suddenly things had turned ugly.

"Goddamn it, you clumsy bitch! Look what you made me do to my husband!"

May had been mortified. Frankie's laughter had started to subside, and she sobered slightly at Marilyn's boorish behavior. Jack was doing his traditional slow burn.

"I want an apology," Marilyn yelled in May's face, "right fucking now! And another round of drinks, on the goddamn house."

Frankie had scooted across the seat to reach out to Marilyn.

"Marilyn, that's enough. It wasn't her fault."

Marilyn had yanked her arm away at Frankie's touch, then slowly turned to face her. May had scurried for cover. The two standing women had faced off as Jack watched from his seat.

Marilyn's anger had mounted, "Who the hell asked you, Frankie?"

Before they could come to blows, Jack had jumped in, "Both of you sit down and shut the fuck up."

May seated Farrell and Frankie in a booth, then handed them menus.

"I never got to thank you for standing up for me, Frankie."

"I'm sorry about that whole night. All three of us had way too much to drink. Both of them can get pretty mean when they're drunk."

"They don't have to be drunk to get pretty mean.

But they haven't been in here since." She smiled. "So, what can I bring you to start?"

Frankie looked over at Farrell. "Gin and tonics?"

He nodded, "How are the steaks?"

"Good."

"Two steaks. Make mine medium rare."

"Mine, too."

May took back the menus, "You got it."

A Patsy Cline song welled up out of the jukebox as May headed back into the kitchen. Farrell smiled at Frankie.

"What?"

"You want to dance?"

"This is slow dancing, cheek-to-cheek music." She suddenly felt shy. "I can't dance that way. I haven't since —"

"Come on. I won't get mad if you step on my toes."

She stared at him a couple of seconds coloring slightly. "All right...show me what you can do."

They stood, moved together and very slowly began to float across the dance floor. Farrell glanced at his feet a couple of times as his confidence built. Frankie smiled, her movements fluidly graceful, effortless. After a minute or so, she put her head on his shoulder.

"You sure smell good. What perfume is that?"

"I'm not wearing any," Frankie smiled wickedly, "Hormones. I'm pre-menstrual. That's probably what you smell. It can come on strong with me. It's not the first time someone has mentioned it."

Farrell laughed softly, "You are too much."

6

The sign, *Rich Man's Burden*, flashed in neon over the entrance to the strip club.

Frankie crossed the street, took one last drag, then tossed her spent cigarette in the gutter as she approached the doors.

Inside, there was a long line of blue and black light behind the narrow bar. A sensual funky sex ballad, *"Lone Ranger"* by Betty Davis welled up out of the cavernous expanse.

Young dark-haired stripper Valerie Richman gyrated provocatively to the music, her back to the bar and 13 patrons.

Frankie parked herself on a stool as Moe, the bartender with rasta dreads, high-fived her.

"If it isn't Frankie 'Five African' Powers, herself. The policewoman with the mystical light shining out of her – so bright it blinds you."

Frankie laughed, in spite of her depressed state,

"For a Jamaican you got a helluva lot of Irish in you."

"What'll you have Detective Powers?"

"The regular."

He held up a bottle of Stoli, then poured a double when she nodded. A song by Girlschool, *"Baby Doll"*, blasted from the PA. The lime green and lavender stripes of neon that framed the liquor bottles in the wall shelves behind the counter were starting to give Frankie a head-ache, so she turned to face the stage. Her smile went from genuine good humor to angry frustration as she recognized who was onstage.

Valerie undulated suggestively in an inferno of red and yellow lights as one of the patrons slipped a ten dollar bill into her G string. Frankie turned sideways, looking down at her newly-arrived drink. At first she pushed it away from her, but after a few seconds, she grabbed it and gulped it down.

She suddenly waded through the sweaty men clustered around the front of the dance floor's pit, then strode purposefully up, leapt onto the stage, grabbed Valerie by one wrist and dragged her towards the wings in one continuous motion. The strobe lights went on as Valerie yanked herself away but slipped, falling to her ass. Frankie took hold of Valerie's mane of hair, and Valerie clamped onto Frankie's forearm as she was hauled backwards. Hoots and catcalls from the audience welled up over the girl band metal. Responding to the commotion, clad-in-black Cal Nero and night manager Jay Hellinger emerged from the office door to watch. They gave each other a sidelong glance.

Right before Frankie and Valerie reached backstage, a burly, bearded bouncer made a foolish attempt to block Frankie. Without stopping, Frankie coldcocked him, sending him into the laps of two seated patrons.

In the dressing room, three strippers made themselves scarce as Frankie tossed Valerie into their midst. Without warning, night manager Jay was in Frankie's face. Cal Nero lay low in the corridor, lackadaisically leaning against the wall.

"What-the-fuck you think you're doing, Powers? This isn't what Jack pays you for."

Frankie was so pissed she grabbed Jay by the face and sent him flying in reverse into one of the mirrors, breaking it.

"Valerie's underage! She just turned 17 last month. She's Jack's daughter for fuck's sake! Does he know she's down here?"

Jay picked himself up, looking at her with a mingling of fear, hate and new respect. He wiped a trickle of blood from his cheek.

"He–he–knows –"

Valerie sidled up to Frankie, rubbing her sore scalp, "Yeah, he knows. And he thinks it's funny."

Frankie couldn't believe her ears. Her dad Nick's words came back to haunt her. She stared into space for a second then turned to Valerie.

"You, fucking put some clothes on!"

Valerie reluctantly moved over to her stuff, then pulled on a pair of jeans and a denim jacket.

Jay timidly spoke up, "Frankie, Jack's going to want to –"

Frankie put up her hand to silence him, "Don't even start that shit." She grabbed Valerie's arm. "Come on, I'm taking you out of here."

Cal, laughing softly, barred their way as they moved out through the club.

"Hey, Frankie. What's the problem, honey?"

"Don't 'honey' me, you sonofabitch."

"Calm down, girl, I'm on your side."

"Right. Listen Cal, I don't have time for your smooth-talking-rattlesnake-from-hell routine. Get out of my goddamn way."

Frankie yanked Valerie past him. Valerie was chomping at the bit, resentful of her status as a minor as they headed for the front door. Outside, Valerie wrested herself free of Frankie's iron grip, and Frankie was briefly distracted by the sight of Vince Farrell standing against the wall outside the entrance.

Jimmy Chavez pulled up along the curb in his 1968 convertible GTO, his attention riveted by the unfolding melodrama.

Farrell sensed what was going down, "Everything okay?"

"Yeah. Everything's fine." Valerie's tone went from sarcastic to venomous as she directed her anger at Frankie, "You goddamn hypocrite! The only time you give a shit about underage girls is when they're your own flesh and blood. What about all the other girls that've come through this town my age and younger that've worked this place? Hunh? Girls strung out and cracked back."

Frankie became defensive, "I don't know about any other underage girls. I've always taken your dad's word for it before. So I never checked."

"You never checked. That's 'cause my sonofabitch dad pays you not to check."

She spat at Frankie's feet, then walked briskly off, vaulting into Jimmy's front seat. He revved the car, burned rubber and peeled down the boulevard. Within seconds they had disappeared.

"Let them go?"

Frankie stared at Farrell, "Yeah. Let 'em go…Let 'em go to hell." Alarm bells started going off in her head, "What-the-fuck are you doing here? Checking up on me?"

"As a matter of fact I am."

She was taken back by his candor. She crossed the street to her car, and Farrell kept pace with her. Unlocking the driver's door, she whirled around to face him.

"Who for? Torres?"

He locked eyes with her. They stared into each other's souls in uneasy silence. Finally, she broke contact and swung gracefully into the car seat, slamming the door so abruptly he was barely able to get out of the way. She rolled down the window.

"It figures. Sweet Home's too small to have an Internal Affairs. Stands to reason he'd have to bring in someone from outside. I'm just surprised he didn't go to Palm Springs or Riverside"

She revved the engine and suddenly roared away. Farrell stood in the middle of the street, gazing after her. Just as suddenly she screeched to a halt, shifted into reverse and careened back to his side. She looked up into his face, not saying a word. Very slowly her angry glare transformed into a mischievous smile.

Farrell's stoic expression melted, and he smiled, too. "What?"

"I had a really good time at dinner with you earlier. It's midnight, and I'm headed home. You want to stop by for a nightcap?"

"Sure. I'll follow you."

Cal and Jay stood in the doorway of the strip club, watching the two finish their conversation and Farrell head for his car. Jay dabbed the side of his mouth with a napkin-wrapped ice cube, then licked a drop of blood that had trickled onto his lip.

7

As they shot down the dark desert highway, the cold air caused Jimmy and Valerie to snuggle close in in the convertible front seat.

"That fucking bitch. She cost me a whole night's tips."

"So what. We're splitting tonight anyway."

"Yeah, but after I'd collected some cash in my gee. At the end of the night.

"Calm the fuck down. I've got a bankroll. This is actually better. We get an early start to Tijuana, and your dad and his goons are less likely to think we're making a run for it."

Valerie turned back to face front, folded her arms and fumed.

Jimmy laughed, "Jesus, lighten up."

"I would have to have a cousin who's a cop. Who's bent and paid off by my scumbag dad."

"You know what I think? She's finally waking up to what's really going on. I could tell by the way she looked when you laid into her. She's been in a stupor ever since her old man and kid got burned up. If she really knew what was going down in this county and didn't care, do you think she would've bothered to wade in and pull you out of there?"

"I can't believe you're taking her side. Since when did you get the degree in psychology? How do you know so much about her?"

"I'm not taking her side. I'm not taking anybody's side. Fuck that. I worked for her dad for a couple months two summers after the fire. When he first got shot and was in the wheelchair. Anytime Frankie was too fucked up to take care of him – which was half the time – I'd go over there to help Nick out. I like him. He's all right. As far as Frankie goes, once you get under all that cynical bullshit of hers, that thick hide, she's probably one of the only ones in town who does give a shit."

"Yeah, well I guess we'll never know. As far as I'm concerned that hole-in-the-wall and everyone in it is history."

He smiled, then burst out laughing. He turned up a punk metal song on the car stereo. She put her arms around his neck and kissed him wetly in the ear. As the music became more frenzied, she climbed on top of him, straddling his lap and reaching down between his legs. They kissed with lusty abandon, and it was all that Jimmy could do to keep his eyes on the road.

There was a star-filled night sky above Jack Richman's sprawling, fifties-vintage ranch house, and it would have been an almost idyllic scene except the chirping crickets were almost drowned out by a blasting stereo on the second floor.

Marilyn Richman was on the phone with one finger

in her ear, trying to hear the person on the other end. She finally blew her stack and turned towards the foyer of the tasteless, decadent homestead. She shouted at the ceiling.

"Vanessa, turn that goddamn shit down. I mean it." She took her hand off the receiver and spoke to her husband on the other end. "Yeah, well she's your goddamn prima donna daughter, Jack. I can't do a fucking thing with her. Speaking of which, you get a line yet on her bitch sister?" The music upstairs finally went off. Vanessa very carefully picked up her bedroom extension with her hand over the mouthpiece.

Jack's voice dripped sarcasm, "What do you think?"

He was in his El Dorado on his cell phone and was obviously in a malevolent, killing mood. Jay sat silently next to him, the desert racing by outside. "That Chavez kid is out of his mind. I guess he doesn't remember he bought that GTO from me. I never took out the Lojack." He laughed, "Those two are in for a helluva surprise."

When Mariyln spoke in a sing-song voice, Jack could tell she was smiling, "What're you gonna do when you catch up with them, Jack?"

"You'll see. But honey, as far as right now goes, you don't want to know."

Marilyn was getting off on the speculation over the couple's fate, and her imagination was running wild, "Yeah, I do. Come on, tell me."

"Baby, the less you know the better. And I want you to get those other girls out of the Warehouse and off to Vegas tonight."

Marilyn was not happy, "Jack, no. I'm in for the night. Besides none of the usual boys I can trust are around to drive them. Cal has to go back to the club.

"Goddamn it, Marilyn, do what I tell you and fucking do it yourself! There's only three girls, and they're all so fucked up on the smack they'll do anything you tell them."

Back at the house, there was an audible click on the phone. Marilyn turned to look at the ceiling. She slowly headed towards the staircase with the cordless receiver and gestured to Cal who was about ready to walk out the front door.

"Jack –"

"After what I do tonight, there may be some heat. Plus you heard what Cal and Jay said about Frankie getting uppity at the club earlier. I swear to Christ she's starting to go through the same thing her goddamn husband went through, getting a conscience once she figures out how deep she's in. Then to top it off, her cozying up to the undercover narc Torres brought in from Bakersfield. I've got a feeling some shit may come down. I want to be more than ready for anything. Leave now and you can be back before dawn."

Marilyn tried again to get a word in edgewise, "Jack –"

"Goddamn it! Just do it!"

He hung up on her, and Marilyn clicked off the phone as she rounded the corner into Vanessa's bedroom with Cal close behind her.

As soon as Vanessa spotted the pair she became a deer frozen in the headlights, unable to hang up her extension. Marilyn pulled a syringe and a tiny metal case full of heroin out of a case in her leather jacket. Cal advanced towards Vanessa, blocking her path around the bed.

"What're you doing?"

Marilyn sat down at Vanessa's desk and began to prepare a shot. "Bring her over here."

8

Valerie fell asleep with her head on Jimmy's shoulder as they drove across the border into Tijuana. She came awake with a start as they pulled into the parking lot of a rundown motel.

"Nice. Keep showing me the good life, baby."

"Hey, watch your mouth, Val, it's just for a few hours. I'm too beat to drive any further."

"What time is it?"

"A little after four, I think. We made good time."

She lit a cigarette as he jumped out and went to check in at the shabby office.

Frankie and Vince Farrell danced cheek-to-cheek in the candlelight of her living room. Al Green crooned low and sexy on the stereo as they wafted down the hall into the bedroom.

They kissed each other, and the kiss became an all-encompassing embrace as they helped each other out of their clothes and sank back onto the unmade bed.

Jimmy and Valerie made love in the shadows of the funky motel room. Flashing, lurid yellow and lavender neon pulsed through the room every few seconds.

Jack Richman's El Dorado pulled slowly up in the alley outside the motel office. He stopped as he spotted the GTO parked against the building. He lit a cigarette, glanced at Jay seated beside him, then drove slowly off again.

Frankie was losing herself in the lovemaking. It seemed that, all too soon, grey light was prying its way through the drawn curtains over the bedroom window. With that first hint of dawn, Frankie sat up in bed, the sheet falling below her breasts, and she clicked her Zippo to light a cigarette. Just as she had gotten lost in the sex, Frankie became lost in the azure fire of the lighter, till the faint hint of dawn was nothing but a welter of cold blue flame. The next thing Frankie knew, she was exiting from her back door wrapped in a sheet. Her toughened bare feet navigated the pebbly, prickly ground without discomfort, and she carried a single candle in a silver holder in one hand and an almost empty bottle of vodka in the other. Her cigarette hung lazily from her mouth. She was silhouetted against the hill in front of her as she floated, hypnotized, towards the dawn light. She stopped by a dead and dried-out chainfruit cholla tree at the edge of her yard.

Farrell, clad only in blue jeans, approached from the house and stopped a few feet behind her, watching her as she set the towering seven foot tall cactus shrub on fire with the candle. She tossed the cigarette into the flames, then belted a swig from the bottle. Farrell came up from behind, turned her around and took the bottle from her grasp. He tossed it, then took her in his arms. She dropped the candlestick and snaked her arms around his neck, surrendering to his kiss as the sheet started to slip away. The burning cholla blurred against the blinding sun rising directly behind them.

Valerie rubbed Jimmy's bare chest as he sat on the edge of the bed zipping up his jeans.

"Jimmy, I don't want you to go."

He pulled on his tanktop. "Jeez, Valerie, I'm only going to be gone ten minutes. We're out of smokes. And I want to get a bottle of tequila."

Valerie playfully whispered, "Real men drink mescal, not tequila."

Jimmy grimaced, "Fuck that." He tousled her hair, stood up and made for the door. Just before shutting it on his way out, he turned back to her, grabbing his crotch.

"Keep that warm for me, baby."

"You know I will."

He left.

Jimmy walked past the darkened overhang of a carport. Once he was out of sight, around the corner of the building, Jack emerged from the shadows and the pulsing neon. He threw a look over his shoulder in Jimmy's direction as he headed for their room.

Valerie was lying face down on her pillow as Jack quietly entered. He walked casually over to her bedside and sat down. He, too, playfully tousled her hair, then massaged the back of her neck. She squirmed seductively, purring like a cat.

Her voice was dreamy, full of sex, "That was quick, baby."

"Not quick enough."

Valerie ricocheted around, but Jack grabbed her around the mouth and jaw as she turned, so her screams were stifled. He pinned the back of her head against the pillow and wall. Her eyes went wide in terror, and her attempts at movement were completely frustrated by Jack's iron grip.

"Now what does this remind you of, Val?" He smiled a wicked smile. "I told you what I'd do to you if you ever tried to run away from me again, didn't I?" Jack's eyes were crazy. "Didn't I?"

Valerie struggled in vain as her father choked her to death.

Carrying a small bag, Jimmy fumbled with the key and let himself in. He set the bag down on the edge of the bed. Valerie appeared to be asleep, her face buried in the pillow. He removed the cigarettes, unwrapped them, pulled one out and lit it, all the time watching Valerie. The bag with the tequila pint rolled off the bed, making a loud thud on the dirty linoleum floor.

"Shit!" As he picked it up, he finally realized something strange was going on. He sat down on the edge of the mattress next to his girl and shook her by the shoulder.

"Hey, Val. Val – Val, wake up." He suddenly became worried, "Goddamn it, honey. Wake up." When he turned her over, he saw the bruise marks on her throat and her dead eyes staring sightlessly at the ceiling. Jack reared up behind Jimmy, bringing a sap down on the boy's head.

When Jimmy came to, what he saw in his line of vision was the bottom edge of the bed and Jack's lower half laboring over something on the mattress. Tied with his arms behind his back and a nasty bruise on his temple, he struggled to rise up to see better.

"Goddamn you, Jack! Fucking murdering your own kid!"

Jack's legs loomed large, one cowboy-booted foot kicking squarely at the center of Jimmy's face, breaking his nose. Then Jack stood there with one foot on Jimmy's head.

"Shut up, you goddamn greaser. She knew what would happen if she got rabbit in her blood again. She fucking knew. And she went ahead and defied me anyway."

"You are one sick fuck."

Jack smiled, "Says you." He kicked Jimmy in the face again, then moved back over to the bed and continued wrapping Valerie's corpse in the sheets and the bedspread.

The El Dorado was backed up right to the door. Jay got out and opened the trunk as Jack came out of the room with Valerie's wrapped-up corpse over his shoulder. He tossed it into the trunk like a sack of potatoes.

"Shit. You took the Chavez kid out already? I wanted to see the look on the little prick's face."

Jack just smiled.

"How did Val take it?"

"Not too well."

"Well, where is she? We should get out of here."

Jack laughed softly, "Val's already in the trunk." Shocked in spite of himself, Jay was incredulous, "You whacked Val?"

Jack handed Jay Jimmy's keys. "She's been walking a thin line for a long time. I'd had enough. I've got other plans for Chavez. You go get his car, then pull out and follow me."

9

Just after dawn, Jack Richman's El Dorado flew along the
highway towards the border crossing. It slowed as it fell
into line behind several other cars. Jay pulled up behind
him in Jimmy's convertible.

A border guard approached.

Jack was all smiles, "Hi."

"Good morning. Are you a United States citizen?"

"Yessir. I'm proud as hell to be a U.S. citizen."

"What was the purpose of your trip?"

In the El Dorado trunk, the fully conscious, battered
Jimmy, his mouth gaffers-taped shut and bound hand-and-
foot, lay alongside Valeries blanket-wrapped body. His eyes
darted back-and-forth as he struggled furiously in vain.

"Just pleasure. Overnight."

"Bringing in anything with you?"

A sick grin on his face, Jack showed the guard
the sap that he had used earlier to knock out Jimmy. He
simultaneously produced an official-looking badge.

The guard reached in to take the badge from Jack.

"Oh, wow, reserve sheriff. You should've said something to me earlier. I would've waved you right through. I used to be in the sheriff's reserves up in Maricopa County."

"No, really?"

Suddenly a horn honked several cars back. The border guard glared behind the El Dorado and Jay in the GTO, noticeably perturbed and ready to roust someone.

"The guy behind me in the GTO is a friend."

"That's fine. I guess I better let you both go."

In the trunk, Jimmy shut his eyes in consternation as the car started to pass through the crossing.

"Nice to meet you, Deputy Richman."

Jack smiled a Cheshire cat smile and saluted the guard.

As soon as the after-crossing traffic crush let up, the El Dorado and GTO raced away from the border. Jack began singing another one of his favorite tunes from *Oklahoma.* "Oh, what a beautiful morning/oh, what a beautiful day/I've got a beautiful feeling/everything's going my way…"

Vince Farrell was single, but he had been married twice. His first wife, Carol, he had wed right out of college and just before he entered the police academy. They had been together four years, then his youthful hubris and the macho culture of the police had led him astray. Carol was perfect in a lot of ways, probably too perfect he thought, but then again he was not a believer in 20/20 hindsight. They had had one child, a beautiful daughter who was now nearly 16, who he never got to see anymore because the breakup had so alienated Carol. In the end, his philandering and temporary callousness had caused Carol to begin drinking, something from which she had previously shied away, and she had become severely alcoholic. His second wife, Molly, he knew through the police department. He had known from the beginning she was a drunk and that she was bitter and also just a bit crazy, but that was partly what had attracted him to her. Just as he was sure part of Frankie's obviously nihilistic death-wish-alcoholic-craziness was what was attracting him now. He had had a child with Molly, too, but in the end, Molly had left him for someone else, a sanitation engineer on the east coast, and she had taken their little boy, Terry, with her and moved in with the man while he was supervising a "super-site" clean up of one of the worst toxic waste dumps in the northeastern United States. Son Terry had gradually developed a nasty case of acromegaly, something which had just recently killed him. Farrell put up a better front but, in many ways, he was on a similar trajectory to Frankie, shooting out of orbit and slowly burning up as he got nearer to the sun.

Farrell climbed the steps to Nick Powers' apartment.
        Nick was sitting in his wheelchair staring out the window. Vince knocked on the screen door, then opened it.
        "Can I come in?"
        "You're halfway in already. You might as well go for it and come the rest of the way."
        "I'm Vincent –"
        "– Farrell. I know. You're the guy Torres brought in from Bakersfield to bring down Jack Richman. And maybe take down my baby, Frankie. Am I right?"
        Vince nodded uncomfortably.
        "Well, how about it, tough guy. Are you going to bust Frankie?"
        "I hope the hell not."
        "Why do you say that? Do you really give a damn one way or the other?"
        "When I got here a few days ago, I would've said

no. But now –"

"Now?"

"I don't know. I'm starting to –" He could not finish his sentence. He caught sight of the picture of Frankie and her late husband Rick and son Joey, and he picked it up.

"Do you know anything about Frankie?"

"Yeah, a bit. Torres filled me in."

"That's her husband, Rick, and my little grandson, Joey. They got burned to death in a fire about ten years ago. Rick was a detective working on the force. He was making things hot for Jack. I've always been pretty sure that Jack had something to do with the fire. I've never been able to prove anything. Or that he had anything to do with me getting shot later."

"What does Frankie think?"

"Deep down she must know. But she can't handle it yet. It's too much for her to believe. That her own flesh and blood uncle, her good mother's black sheep brother, who she's known since she was little, would ever do such a thing." He paused and sighed. "She was in a vulnerable state after all that crazy stuff went down. They promoted her from office work to Rick's job because she was the only one in the department who had the training. They wanted to maybe bring in somebody from out of town. I convinced them otherwise. But she'd already gotten cynical and bitter. She let things slide and looked the other way. She knew Jack was recruiting girls for houses in Nevada, that he was moving grass in from Mexico."

Farrell tried to fill in the blanks. "She figured, what-the-fuck difference did it make? Nobody seemed to be getting hurt?

Nick nodded, "Frankie's finally beginning to see there's more going on than she thought. And she's starting to feel things again."

"Things are rising to the surface."

"Yeah, evidence of the wreckage. So you're starting to... what?"

"What do you mean?"

"A couple of minutes ago you said you were starting to ___ about Frankie. What are you starting to do, Vince? Fall in love with my baby?"

Farrell looked away, embarrassed.

"Even if you two have been in the sack, you haven't known her long enough."

Farrell suddenly became indignant, "Tell me, Nick. When you're on a job like mine, like Frankie's, like the one you used to have where there are people who could take you out in a heartbeat, how long do you have to know someone before you know you want to spend the rest of your life with them?"

Nick stared down in his lap, then out of the window.

10

Frankie's car sped up the winding road to Jack and Marilyn's ranch house. She screeched to a halt at the top of the drive and got out, slamming the door as loud as she could. She paused, looked around, then decided to head towards the back of the sprawling, 1950s vintage structure. As she rounded the bend to the back patio, she found Marilyn practicing with her bullwhip on liquor bottles lined up on the edge of an ancient Spanish-fountain.

Marilyn sensed Frankie's presence but didn't turn around, continuing with her antics.

"Well, Frankie! To what do I owe the pleasure?"

"Is Jack here?"

Marilyn stopped, turned to look at her for a few seconds, then shook her head.

"Say, honey, you look a bit flushed. New boy-friend?"

Frankie removed her sunglasses to reveal bloodshot daggers of fire.

"It wouldn't be that narc Manny Torres brought in from Bakersfield, would it? Or is it just the usual hangover?"

Frankie walked to the patio bar in answer and poured herself a stiff one. Marilyn went back to practicing with her bullwhip. The breaking liquor bottles sounded like pistol shots.

"Where is Val?"

"She didn't come home last night. Jack's a bit worried."

"Yeah, I'll just bet he is. Is that why he was letting her strip at the club?"

Marilyn stopped again and turned to face Frankie, getting steamed up. "Jack and I don't like nosy parkers."

"Fuck you, Marilyn, I'm different. I'm a helluva lot closer to Val than you. At least I'm blood kin."

Marilyn put her hands on her hips, stepping closer.

"Frankie, honey, do you know what Jack and I do to folks who can't keep their snouts in their own backyard? And it doesn't matter to us whether they've been swimming in the same gene pool or not."

Frankie gulped down the rest of her drink, set the glass down on the counter and headed back to her car without another word.

Cal Nero drifted out of the house with his silk shirt open. Little Cecilia, bedraggled and barefoot, clung tightly to him as if he were a human life preserver. They stopped alongside Marilyn.

"I'd like nothing better than to mop the floor with that bitch's brains."

Marilyn turned and smiled at him.

"You do have a way with words, Cal. She doesn't change her tune, you may just get your wish."

11

It was almost noon on the empty desert highway. Jack pulled the El Dorado to the roadside, and Jay stopped behind him. Jack walked briskly to the GTO.

"Help me get them into your car. Open your trunk." Jay disembarked, popped the lid and then met Jack as he opened the El Dorado trunk. Jack lifted out Valerie's body.

Jack deposited Valerie in Jay's arms. Jay shivered at the coldness of her touch and dead weight.

"Take Val and stash her in the back. I'll get Chavez."

Jay carried the body to the GTO.

Jack bent over the tied-up Jimmy Chavez in the El Dorado trunk. "Torres'll never believe you anyway, but if you try to breathe a word of what really happened, your mama's history."

Jimmy tried to struggle as Jack reached for him and, without hesitation, Jack brought the sap down again on his skull. Jack picked up and carried Jimmy's unconscious form to the driver's seat of the GTO. Jay slammed the trunk and joined him. Jack quickly untied Jimmy's hands and legs, ripped the tape off of his mouth, then poured some of the tequila over the boy's battered face. He tossed the bottle on the GTO floor.

"Okay, we're going to release the brake and push the car over into that yucca."

They labored furiously to send the GTO careening into the dried-up cactus. Once accomplished, Jack dialed the sheriff's office on his cell phone, then handed it to Jay.

"Tell them you were driving along when you spotted an accident, then hang up before they can ask your name."

Frankie sat at her desk flipping through the pages of a file of missing teenage girls from around California. There was a knock on the door.

"Come in."

Farrell peeked around the door, then slipped into the room. "I've got some bad news. Jimmy Chavez cracked up his GTO not too far outside town. They found him drunk and unconscious. Knox is bringing him in any minute."

"And? How about Val?"

Farrell was hesitant, "I'm sorry —"

Frankie stood up anxiously. "What, goddamn it?"

"Wrapped up in a blanket in the trunk — Knox thinks she was strangled."

Frankie's expression was stoic, but the news hit her hard. She slowly got up and walked out. Farrell followed her down the hall, then outside into the still fiery late afternoon sun.

Frankie went up to her car and leaned against it. She put on her sunglasses and looked off down the street. Farrell tentatively moved closer to her. A tear rolled down Frankie's cheek.

"I don't understand..."

Suddenly Knox's patrol car whipped around the corner and pulled diagonally to the curb. Knox jumped out, glanced at Farrell and Frankie as he frantically ripped open the back door and yanked handcuffed Jimmy from the backseat. Farrell and Frankie stared at them in silence. Jimmy glared insanely at Frankie until he disappeared inside the building. Before either of them could say anything, Jack Richman and Jay Hellinger screeched to a halt in the middle of the street. Jack leapt from the car, expertly feigning a father's tearful rage. Farrell moved quickly to intercept him.

"Where is that motherfucker! I'm going to kill him! I'm going to strangle him just like he did my baby!"

Jay edged his way up to help push struggling Jack back to his car. Jack spotted Frankie.

"What-the-fuck, Frankie, I want to see that fucking asshole kid! Now!"

Frankie managed to keep her emotions in check. "You can't see him, Jack. He's got to be booked. I'm very sorry about Valerie."

Jack raged at the sky, "Fuck! Fuck! FUCK!"

He let Jay place him back in the El Dorado. Jay gave Frankie a dirty look as he ran around the side, dove behind the wheel then, revving the engine, blasted off. Frankie and Farrell stared after the cloud of dust for a few seconds. Frankie looked down at the gutter, then headed back into the building.

12

Jay hadn't bargained for this much killing. He instinctively knew more was in the works and, sure enough, as soon as they left the vicinity of the sheriff's department, Jack got a call from Marilyn about a girl who'd outlived her usefulness at the Warehouse. She was as strung out as could be without overdosing, and she was proving too hard to handle. Marilyn had called Jack because he personally liked to take care of the problem girls.

Jay asked himself if it hadn't been Valerie who had just been snuffed a few hours before, someone he knew fairly well, someone he actually kind of liked and was attracted to, if it had just been the Chavez kid, if that would have gotten to him in the same way. Then, too, Jack strangling to death his own daughter – somehow it changed his opinion of his boss. He had always liked Jack Richman before, both because of and in spite of his sadistic sense of humor. Jay had been working for him since he was a teen-ager, when his own dad, Morgan J. Hellinger, a

peculiarly adept mob attorney, had still been alive and
representing two thirds of the organized crime figures in
Southern California's Inland Empire. First Jay had wanted
to go to law school and be a "mouthpiece" like his old man.
Then, in high school, he saw the amount of bookwork and
writing and memorizing it was going to take and came to
the conclusion that maybe he wasn't cut out for the practice
of law after all. He had dropped out of high school not too
long after that realization. His dad Morgan hadn't cared one
way or another. By that time he was battling lung cancer,
a virulent strain resulting from smoking sometimes three
packs of cigarettes a day and up to ten cigars on the week-
ends. When Morgan shuffled down six feet under, Jay had
already been working the door at Jack's strip club and
helping out with the odd jobs around the Warehouse for a
good 15 months.

Up until recently, he had not been aware of the
"disposal routine" as it had come to be known around some
segments of the Richman household. Girls who got rabbit
in their blood or got to greedy with the drugs or who
overdosed themselves on purpose or accidentally, or
perhaps even suffered the slings and arrows of some
outrageous high roller's overly aggressive perversion, thus
necessitating discreet removal of all record of their earthly
existence. Now he knew about it quite unlike anything else
he had ever known before in his whole life. And he found
he didn't like it. He didn't like it at all.

But he was still working for Jack. It wasn't as if he
could just leave. He was not the sharpest tool in the shed,
as the saying went, but he was sharp enough to realize that
Jack would make mincemeat out of him if he so much as
voiced an inadvertent squeamish squeak of displeasure.
Jack would not care in the least if he was the son of a long
time dead friend who had kept him – Jack – out of both
state and federal hoosegows more times than he could

count on two hands.

After all, look what Jack had done to his own flesh and blood little girl.

When they got to the Warehouse, Jack was upset to find May Fossett had already gone the way of all flesh. Too much heroin and crack in one 12 hour period. Marilyn had misjudged the situation, something which would give her cause to judge herself even more harshly than would Jack. May was newly-wrapped in an old army blanket and ready for removal to The Pit.

Jay didn't want to go, but Jack was in a bad mood and, perhaps picking up on the vibes of Jay's newly delicate sensibilities, had decided Jay was just the man to drive him and May to her final resting place deep in the mountain cradle of sulphurous rock a few miles distant.

When they got there, Jay was not only appalled by the smell but by the vision – an image of a sweltering, steaming stone crater filled with decaying, human female carrion. At least 20 bodies in various states of decomposition lay under the broiling desert sun. Well-hidden up a nearly impassable dirt road, a forgotten burial ground, a cauldron of putrefying flesh, it was too much for any normal human being to bear. Too make matters worse, springs of popping, hellish liquid sulphur bubbled and spurted in irregular pockets dotting the perimeter of The Pit.

Jack roughly nudged Jay, and Jay realized Jack had been talking to him, and he hadn't heard a word. And at this, Jack was not happy. Jay finally realized Jack wanted him to take one end of the army blanket sling that held the girl's corpse, and he did so reluctantly. Before he could protest, Jack was swinging the girl back in forth, as if it was a game and she was in a hammock.

"I'm going to count three. On three, let her go."

Jay couldn't answer, only gulped and nodded.

"One – two – THREE!" They let her go, and her body flailed stiff but somehow fishlike into the soup of bloated dead flesh.

Jay was suddenly on his knees, puking his guts out. He thought of Cal and Cal's stories, and how he had always thought Cal sure had a sick sense of humor and had to be joking about this teen slut burial ground they called The Pit.

Jack was disgusted with Jay, so kicked him in the ass and sent him flying.

Jay's first impression of the touch of the mess of death was of landing on a wet, incredibly stinking air mattress. Obscene gases were wafting up from beneath him as he stumbled to his feet. He felt as if his reason was going. Gaining the lip of the perimeter, he tripped, hopped, skipped away from Jack, shuffling about trying to avoid falling into one of the sulphur springs. Images from his youth, fairy tale characters and religious icons, were appearing in front of him, and he felt himself much like an angel dancing on the head of the proverbial pin. It was an indelible image he couldn't chase from his mind – right up until the second Jack shot him from 15 feet away in the base of his skull.

Knox was fingerprinting a barely-able-to-stand Jimmy Chavez. Shelley, a female deputy, waited behind the counter for the process to finish. Torres walked out of his office at the same time Frankie entered. His eyes were on her, but her gaze was riveted on Jimmy.

Knox roughly threw Jimmy towards the corridor leading to the jail cells, tossing the fingerprint page to Shelley with his other hand.

"Knox, take it easy," Torres shouted.

Shelley was confused. "What should I put as the charge?"

Torres looked at Frankie and reluctantly answered,

"Better put down murder for the time being. Where did they take Valerie?"

Shelley looked at a post-it note. "Hospital morgue. Danny Suzuki's supposed to be towing Jimmy's GTO to one of the garages out back."

Farrell came in and joined Torres as Frankie pivoted, slowly following after Knox and Jimmy. She twisted and turned down several seemingly endless corridors. Finally she reached the cell area. Knox had already deposited Jimmy into one and was locking the door. He gave Frankie an exasperated look as he headed back to the office section.

Frankie walked up to the bars. Jimmy was sitting on the edge of the bunk, his head back against the wall. He stared into space.

"You going to tell me what happened?"

Jimmy wouldn't even acknowledge her.

"Jimmy, I think you're a cocky fucking asshole. But I can't believe you killed Valerie."

Jimmy, in a great deal of pain, slowly turned his head, "You want to know what happened? Get my mom somewhere safe. Then I'll tell you what went down with Val."

Frankie gripped the bars, "Did Jack have something to do with it?"

Jimmy turned away, his voice cracking, "Get my mom somewhere safe. I'm not telling you anything till then."

Frankie left.

Jimmy put his head in his hands.

Frankie burst out the door of the building with Vince Farrell following close behind. She stopped at her car.

"What's going on, Frankie?"

"I'm not sure. I think Jimmy's in a frame."

"Who by? Jack?"

"I don't know. Probably. Listen, what I have to do right now, I have to do by myself. I'll see you before it gets dark.

She climbed into the car, started to shut the door then opened it again as an afterthought.

"Do me a favor, Vince. Don't say anything to Manny about what I think until I've got more to go on."

Farrell nodded. She closed the door, then backed out the car and zoomed off down the street.

Frankie pulled out her cell phone as she drove and dialed a number.

"Dad, it's me. Listen – No, Dad, listen I don't have time to talk about that stuff now. I need your help on something – Can you keep Jimmy Chavez's mom at your apartment for just a couple of days? Till I find some place more permanent?"

She paused, listening, "Goddamn it, you've got the dirtiest mind. I'll explain when I see you. I need to have her somewhere safe. Somewhere that only I know about – yeah, okay. I don't know how easy it's going to be to convince her. Hopefully we'll be over there in an hour or two. Okay, yeah. Later."

13

By the time Frankie finished her mission of mercy and pulled up in front of the sheriff's building, she was dog-tired.

Frankie passed Shelley at the front desk, then crooked her finger at Vince Farrell as she passed his open door. He got up and followed her into her office. She shut the door behind him.

"What's all the mystery? Where have you been?"

"I had to get Jimmy's mom to a safe place. He said he wouldn't talk to me until that happened. It was a nightmare and a half because I had to tell her what went down. Then she wanted to come and see him right away. It was hell convincing her she would have to wait a day or two to talk to him."

"I wish you'd fill me in on the full picture."

"How can I when I don't know it myself? I've got to talk to Jimmy as soon as possible."

"Well, the way things are now, you're going to have

to be patient until tomorrow."

"What?"

"Calm down. Manny put him in the lockdown ward at the county hospital for overnight observation. Besides seeming a tad suicidal, his skull and face were pretty banged up. Nobody's talking to him tonight. He's under heavy sedation."

Frankie sank down against her desk, deflated.

"Shit."

"If he's okay, they'll bring him back over in the morning. They don't exactly have the facilities for prisoners over there. Knox and one of the other boys have to watch him in shifts."

There was an uncomfortable silence.

"Frankie, I'm sorry about Valerie."

"Has anybody heard from Jack since his award-winning performance earlier?"

"Not a peep."

Frankie suddenly became lost in thought.

"Listen, why don't we go get dinner?"

"I'd rather have a drink."

"Yeah, I'm sure you would. But when was the last time you had any solid food? You should eat, baby."

Frustrated and annoyed, she turned away, "YOu sound like my father."

"Why don't you go on home? I'll go get some food and bring it over.

She nodded and stood with a Herculean effort. "The Mexican place down at the end of the street is good. Don't go to the diner. They're only okay for breakfast."

She started to walk out the door, but Farrell grabbed her hand to stop her.

"Hey –"

She gave him a wistful smile in answer and leaned over to kiss him. They looked into each other's eyes for a

couple of seconds, then she left. He was overcome with a
barrage of warring thoughts. He started down the hall.

"Hey, Vince, come in here a sec."

Farrell popped his head into the open door of
Manny Torres office. The sheriff had his feet up on his
desk.

"What's going on with Frankie?"

"You said yesterday you didn't know if she was
going to drown or come up for air, right? Well, I think she's
coming up for air."

Torres looked away, troubled.

"Vince, you know this is a really small town.
Everybody here is under a microscope. There aren't too
many secrets."

"Get to the point, Manny. As if I didn't know."

"I'm already hearing rumors about you and Frankie."

Farrell stared down at the floor, trying not to lose
his temper.

"Manny, I trust her. You're going to have to be
satisfied with that for now."

"Okay, let's drop it. Listen, I want you to go out
tomorrow to do some surveillance on that place Richman
calls the Warehouse. If you really do trust Frankie, take her
along."

"All right."

Frankie pulled up and very slowly got out of her car,
feeling every bone in her body. She paused in her front yard
for several minutes, listening to the sounds of insects and
other wild life as twilight became night. She stared into the
distance, hypnotized by the desert wilderness. Finally she
headed into the house.

Frankie was sprawled on the couch in candlelight, one
arm across her eyes and the other holding a drink balanced

on her stomach. Low funky soul music played on the FM
stereo. She tried to remember who it was and at last
recognized Otis Redding's dulcet tones. There was a
knock at the screen door.

"Vince?"

"Yeah –" He opened the door and came in.

"All the weird things happening, I was starting to
get worried about you."

She sat up as he joined her on the sofa. He put down
a bag with take-out containers on the cluttered coffee table.

"Hungry yet? I got some tacos."

"I still don't have any appetite. I keep thinking
about Val."

"The thing I'm wondering is –"

"– how Vanessa's doing?

He nodded.

Frankie finished off her drink, "I know. I've been
thinking about her off and on since we saw Jack outside the
station. I wish I could get her out of their house, have her
come and stay here with me." She opened the bag, fished
out a taco and unwrapped it. She forced herself to eat,
then, once finished, gulped down another iced double of
bourbon. A queasy expression bloomed on her face, and she
sank back into the crook of Farrell's arm. A few minutes
passed, and she sat up on the edge of the sofa. Suddenly she
headed for the bathroom. Farrell looked after her, and he
heard the sound of her being sick.

After a few seconds, she reappeared at the edge of
the hall.

"I'm wiped out, Vince. I think I'm just going to
crash. You're welcome to stay if you want, but I'm not
going to be much fun."

He came over to her, put his arm around her
shoulders and steered her into the bedroom. She delicately
removed her outer clothes, then climbed beneath the sheet

in her bra and panties. Vince lay down next to her in a spoon position, propped himself up on one elbow and gently caressed her hair.

She closed her eyes as Vince lovingly stroked her, surrendering to the delicious feeling of having someone care about her.

At dawn, Farrell, already dressed, tried to be as quiet as possible so as not to wake Frankie. Before he left, he placed a note on the nightstand.

14

Farrell was parked on a dirt mountain road and disembarked with a pair of binoculars around his neck. He gradually crouched down as he reached the rise. A large canyon was visible over his shoulder, and Jack Richman's drug and sex slave Warehouse was square in the middle. Farrell checked his watch. It was nearly 7:00 AM. He brought up the binoculars.

A half an hour or so later, a Mustang swerved to a stop in a cloud of dust, and Cal and Marilyn piled out. They reached into the backseat and yanked forth an incapacitated Vanessa and Cecilia from either side. Marilyn held Vanessa by one arm and kicked her in the ass when she didn't move fast enough into the Warehouse interior. Cal and Cecilia followed.

Disgusted, Farrell muttered, "Jesus Christ," under his breath. Approximately 10 minutes passed.

Marilyn and Cal reappeared with Cecilia, climbed into the Mustang and zoomed away. Farrell decided to head back to his car.

A minute later and half a mile away, he was driving on the winding mountain road.

Cecilia suddenly appeared on the pavement ahead, just around the bend, running towards his car. He slammed on the brakes and swerved to avoid hitting her, and she collapsed near the cliff edge. Farrell jumped out and headed towards her crumpled form.

Cal materialized behind him from nowhere. Farrell sensed his presence at the last second, whirled and just missed being bashed over the head with a tire iron. He plucked out his holstered automatic, but Cal knocked it from his grasp. The two struggled in a desperate clench that mushroomed into a full blown, brutal fistfight. Cal climbed on top of Farrell and tried to choke him with the tire iron. Farrell threw him off and both dove for the gun that was teetering on the crumbly brink of the cliff edge. Finally Farrell grasped it and leveled it at Cal. There was the loud snap of slapping cowhide as a black-leather-clad Marilyn appeared from behind an outcropping with her bullwhip. The automatic spun from Farrell's hand. Cal quickly grabbed it and covered him. Cecilia dashed to Cal's side and the shelter of one comforting arm. Farrell gave her a disgusted look, angry with himself for being deceived. Marilyn folded and caressed her whip, smiling a wicked smile.

"Whoa, Ceci, looks like us weak womenfolk can rest easy. Chivalry is not dead – even when it comes to crack whores."

Cecilia was stung by the cruel remark, and Cal proved uncharacteristically protective. "Shut up, Marilyn."

Marilyn joined them as they redirected their attention to Farrell standing alone on the rocky brink.

"Shut up yourself, Cal. Let's do what we came up here for and pluck this thorn from our side."

Cal waved the gun at Farrell, gesturing for him to head to his car, and Farrell followed his directions, moving ahead of him. Just as they reached the driver's side, Cal struck out with his gun hand, knocking Farrell unconscious and depositing him sprawled in the driver's seat. The car was still approximately 10 yards from the sheer drop. Cal let out the emergency brake, then straightened up, shouting at Marilyn.

"It's too much of a rise to push it by myself. You're going to have to get your Mustang and nudge him over the edge."

"All right."

Farrell was out cold, his head resting on the back of the seat, and a stream of blood slowly trickled down his temple.

Marilyn's Mustang approached and, all at once, there was the bang of metal. Farrell's head jerked and lolled as Marilyn began pushing. He slowly came awake, realized what was happening and, in one fluid motion, turned on his ignition. He threw the shift into reverse, and there was the sound of two engines roaring, gears grinding together in a test of opposing strength.

Marilyn was angry as hell, fighting to not lose any ground to the accelerating-in-reverse Farrell. "Damn him!" The vehicles rocked back and forth, to and fro from the brink.

Farrell's face was set in grim determination as he fought for his life.

Marilyn's face glowed with intensity in a demonic mask.

Farrell realized he was losing ground. The car started to go over the edge, and he understood he was going to die.

Marilyn's face contorted sadistically in a grotesquely joyful and triumphant smile.

Farrell's car plummeted over and down to the canyon floor far below. There was a deafening crash, and the vehicle caught fire on impact.

Frankie came abruptly awake from a nightmare. She immediately saw Vince Farrell's note on the bedstand. Groggily, she sat up, propping herself on one elbow and reached for it.

Honey, I wanted to let you sleep. I had to do something for Manny. I'll call you later, xxxoo Vince

Frankie set the note down, and the phone rang. She anxiously reached to the floor and plucked up the receiver.

"Yeah?"

She sat bolt upright, swinging her feet around, her face suddenly grimly set. She shut her eyes tightly as someone told her about Vince Farrell.

The sheriff impound garage towed what was left of Farrell's twisted, burnt-out car into the alley behind the sheriff's building. Frankie stood near the open garage door, her arms folded and sunglasses on.

She crouched down to study Farrell's bumper, then lifted her sunglasses up to reveal reddened eyes. There were visible scrape marks where Marilyn's car had slammed into the chrome. Frankie straightened as Torres stopped beside her and angrily took her by the arm.

"I want to see you in my office. Now!"

She instinctively yanked away. "Get your hands off me, Manny!"

He backed off.

"Where were you when this happened? You were supposed to be with him."

"What are you talking about?"

"When was the last time you talked to Vince?"

Frankie was trying not to break down.

"Last night. I got sick. He stayed over and looked after me. When I woke up this morning, I found a note. It said he didn't want to wake me, that he had to do something for you, and that he'd call me later. I read the note when I woke up. Two seconds later you called."

"Well, you see Frankie I've got a bit of a problem with you right now. I told Vince to go out and do some surveillance on Jack's Warehouse, to take you along if he felt he could really trust you. But you didn't go with him. And now he's fucking dead."

Frankie turned away from Torres and brought her sunglasses back down from her forehead to hide her teary eyes.

Torres sighed. "Against my better judgment, Frankie, I feel in my gut you didn't know about this. That is the only reason I'm not going to suspend you."

She remained completely stoic except for a tear running down her cheek.

"You don't look good, Frankie."

She was suddenly indignant. "Tell me, Manny, how should I look? I just had my teenage cousin, Val, and the guy I've been closest to in the last 10 years murdered. All since yesterday morning. How should I fucking look?" Torres reddened and walked away.

Frankie waited impatiently in Sweet Home High School's administration office. She leaned on the counter while two clerks conferred on the far side of the room. They gave her a dubious look, and one returned to give her information.

"Vanessa Richman hasn't been in class the last two days."

Frankie perched her sunglasses atop her forehead.

"Has anyone called their house?"

"Yes, her stepmother Marilyn said she was under the weather."

Frankie stalked out.

It was late afternoon, the sun disappearing behind a rain cloud as Frankie's car swerved to a halt in a cloud of dust before the Warehouse's entrance. She made her way to the corrugated metal and pounded on it. Cal Nero opened the door next to the garage gate.

"Well, if it isn't one of my favorite sheriff's detectives."

"I need to speak to Jack, Cal. Right fucking now. I've already been up at the house. I couldn't raise anybody."

Cal was overly friendly.

"Hell, Frankie, that's probably because nobody was at home. Jack and Marilyn both went into Vegas. I'm not sure when they'll be back. They wanted to get away for a couple days before Val's funeral."

Upstairs, Jack stood listening to the conversation, watching Frankie and Cal on a closed circuit security monitor.

"What about Vanessa? She hasn't been in school for two days."

"She's probably with Jack and Marilyn."

"You better listen good, Cal, because this is about your sorry ass, too. You tell Jack I know he had Vince Farrell killed –"

Cal feigned surprise, "Farrell's dead?"

"Don't fucking say a word till I'm done! I know Jack and Marilyn and you had something to do with it. And I know Jimmy Chavez is getting framed for Valerie. That one of you sick fucks whacked her, too. I just don't have any proof." She paused, taking a deep breath, "Let me amend that. I don't have any proof – yet. Just make sure Jack knows I'm going to find some no matter how hard I have to dig to get it."

Vanessa was watching, too, through the one way window of the soundproofed second story, but she couldn't hear what they were saying. She was too high on her force-fed drugs to notice Frankie's angry expression, but she studied the scene as Frankie got in her car and peeled out, zooming soundlessly into the wilderness.

Vanessa was stretched out on an old sofa, and she let her head sink back down onto an armrest. Marilyn sat beside her. She siphoned up heroin into a syringe from a spoon on the coffee table. Her black bullwhip lay conspicuously nearby.

"Don't tell me you were getting your hopes up about cousin Frankie."

Even in her numbed out state, Vanessa was horrified.

"She's on our side. Yesterday she even set up her new boyfriend so we'd have an easier time taking him out."

Jack appeared in the background over Marilyn's shoulder as Marilyn shot the smack into Vanessa's bruised arm. Vanessa was listless with despair.

"Don't be poisoning the child's mind, Marilyn –" he laughed, "– that's my job."

Vanessa closed her eyes as Marilyn joined in the cruel mirth.

Jack sauntered leisurely out of the room and joined Cal in the hallway.

"You heard all that shit Frankie was laying down?"

Jack nodded, "I don't think the Chavez kid talked yet. All the same, maybe we should try to get to him tonight. I should have just bashed his head in yesterday, made it look like he died in the accident. But I wanted him to suffer."

"Too late now."

"Torres will be gone after seven. Knox'll probably be on duty which will make it a piece of cake. Arrange the details."

"My pleasure."

15

Frankie pulled into her driveway. She slowly climbed out
of the car and entered the house.

She felt like an infinitesimally microscopic dot in
the universe as she sank back onto the unmade bed. She
threw one arm over her eyes, and her body was wracked
with nearly soundless weeping. Gradually she got it under
control, and the sobbing subsided. Suddenly there was an
audible hiss. Frankie froze for a second, then very slowly
lowered her arm, her eyes darting to the left of her.
A rattlesnake slowly stuck its head out from under the
other pillow. Frankie rolled off the bed in the opposite
direction, throwing the blanket over the snake in one fluid,
continuous motion, wrapping it up so it couldn't escape.
She carried the wadded-up bedclothes into the bathroom
then threw them into the tub. She immediately drew her
gun and pumped lead into the writhing elastic shape
beneath the blanket. The echoing gunshots had her ears
ringing, and the undulations ceased as blood seeped onto

the white enamel.

Out of breath, Frankie sank to a sitting position on the floor against the doorjamb.

It was hours after dark, approaching 1 AM, when Frankie pulled up, quickly disembarked and entered the sheriff's building.

Only one light was on. No one seemed to be around. Frankie stepped lightly with some trepidation, as if even here she was not safe. She padded through the reception area into a large office with several desks. The overhead fluorescent light flickered. Still no one. She continued through and into a maze of corridors leading to the jail cells.

There were five cubicles, four empty. Frankie walked down to the last one, Jimmy Chavez's. At first, she couldn't see him.

"Jesus, don't tell me he's still in the hospital."

There was movement on the floor at the far end of the cot. Jimmy stood up unsteadily and emerged out of the shadows.

"They brought me back all right. But that lame asshole Knox has completely disappeared." He came to the bars.

"Your mom is safe. Now tell me what happened with you and Val."

He looked off dreamily, staring fixedly into space.

"She and I were trying to go somewhere to start fresh. I figured if we laid low in Tijuana for a couple of months, Jack wouldn't find us. I didn't know how crazy he really is. I'd bought that GTO from him. He still had the anti-theft system in the chassis. That's how he found us. I came back to the motel room –" He suddenly could not speak.

After a few seconds, Frankie tried a soothing tone,

"It's okay, take your time, Jimmy."

He angrily wiped away tears.

"I came back to the room after getting some smokes. I –I – I thought Val had finally dropped off. But I could tell something was wrong. When I tried to wake her – her face – she was limp. When her face turned towards me –" He choked up. "Her eyes. God, Frankie, her eyes! They were open and –"

He banged his head against the bars. Frankie reached through to consolingly touch the side of his head.

"It was Jack. He was already waiting in the room for me. He and Jay brought us back up here. Made it look like I'd gotten drunk, killed Val, then crashed my car –"

There was the echoey clanking of someone else moving in the building. Both Frankie and Jimmy instinctively froze and turned their heads in the sound's direction.

"How long has it been since you've seen Knox?"

"I don't know. Maybe an hour. I'm not sure what time it is."

Frankie quietly walked to the entrance of the jail cell corridor. She peered into the guard's lockdown cubbyhole separating the cells from the next hallway. There was a ghostly halo of light shining on the blotter on top of the desk and the cell keys sat in the middle of it.

"Shit!"

She grabbed the keys, drew her .38 with her other hand and made her way back to Jimmy's cell. Jimmy peered between the bars as she unlocked his door.

Frankie whispered, "It's a set up. Knox left the keys out on top of the desk. He never ever does that."

There was another echoey metal clanking far off in the maze of corridors. They both looked in its direction then at each other.

"Jimmy, listen, you're better off staying here. No

one can get into this cell area except the way I've come.
I'm going back out to see what's going on. There's no way
anyone will get past me.

Jimmy was scared. "Unless they fucking waste
you."

Frankie was sure of herself, "That's not going to
happen."

He gave her a doubtful look.

She handed him the keys. "I'll leave these with you.
You see this one –" She held up the largest, "– that's the
key to the door at the end, before the guard desk. You hear
any shooting, lock that door as quick as you can. You'll be
safe until Torres gets back in the morning."

"But –"

"Just do what I tell you. As soon as I'm sure the
building is clear, I'll be back to get you out of here. To
somewhere safe."

Jimmy leaned out of his cell to stare after her as
she glided down the corridor. She cautiously passed into
the guard's little room, then into the next right-angled hall.
She made her way down, her back against the wall and
her gun hand poised. As she reached the corner of the last
bend in the stairs, she paused. She edged around it with
exaggerated caution, beads of sweat standing out on her
wrinkled-with-stress forehead.

Beyond the doorway was the largest office, filled
with desks. There was still the flickering of the fluorescent
light. She inched her way slowly into the deserted area.
A shadowy figure raised a gun to point at the back of her
head, and she froze.

"Jack and I thought you might be paying the
Chavez kid your respects." Frankie recognized Cal's voice.
"It's a good thing I got down here early. Too bad Knox
didn't hang around to help. But the pussy doesn't have any
stomach for the rough stuff." He sighed in mock sympathy,

"Now Frankie this is already hard enough for me. I want you to make it easy on the both of us and turn around very, very slowly."

She started to turn.

"Wait a sec. Drop your gun on the floor ahead of you."

Frankie tossed her .38 onto the linoleum and turned her head slightly to see a steaming coffee pot sitting on a hotplate on the desk to her left. Frankie whipped around, deflecting Cal's automatic which went off once into the pasteboard ceiling and, with her other hand, picked up the glass coffee pot which she smashed into the side of Cal's skull.

He screamed, dropping his gun and holding his face. But the struggle was not over. Frankie went for Cal's Glock, which had landed nearest, but Cal reflexively dove on top of her. His gun slid along the slick surface as both of them crashed to the floor. Both scrambled along horizontally, trying to climb over each other towards the two guns a few feet from them. But their fury served only to knock both weapons further away until they impacted against the elevator that lead to the second floor.

At last, Frankie grabbed Cal's Glock and Cal, Frankie's .38. They bumped against each other, forcing their gun hands up into the air as they both gained their feet. The pressure of Frankie's back against the call button opened the elevator door, and the two spun, falling in. As the door slid shut, both sat on opposite ends pointing their guns at each other. All was suddenly quiet except for the raggedy noise of the two's over-amped lungs trying to catch breath.

Pointing the Glock, Frankie wedged herself into one corner where the door met the wall. Cal pointed the .38 with one hand, trembling with pain as he held the side of his scalded face with the other.

The door suddenly slid open to reveal Jimmy's concerned visage peering in just above Frankie.

Distracted, she shouted. "Jimmy, no."

Cal raised the .38 and shot Jimmy in the face, killing him instantly, and Jimmy promptly fell on top of Frankie as she tried to aim the Glock.

Cal jumped over the two and out of the elevator. Frankie managed to free her gun hand from under Jimmy's dead weight, fire, and wound the fleeing Cal in his left shoulder.

Cal fled out the rear exit, in horrible pain, and Frankie spilled out the door, almost on his heels, running frantically after him.

They careened down deserted alleyways in the sleepy town.

Cal fired once wildly behind him in the hopes of nailing Frankie, but he missed.

Up ahead the glowing embers that were the rear lights of Cal's idling Buick became visible. The passenger door swung open. Only as Cal was about to escape did Frankie stop, take aim and fire the Glock. Cal was hit square in the chest, but he managed to fall inside the car and shut the door. Cecilia in the driver's seat was suitably distraught and looked at him with terror.

Cal was on his last legs. "Go! Go! GO!"

Cecilia snapped out of it, rammed home the gear shift and accelerated.

Frankie watched the car disappear down the highway at high speed. She let her gun hand fall to her side, seriously winded and crouched, looking after the Buick, trying to catch her breath.

Cal's sleek black car was the only vehicle on the road.

He was dying. Cecilia divided her attention between him and the pavement ahead.

He was barely able to speak. "You better – pull over – honey…"

She immediately complied. The Buick rapidly decelerated and spun onto the sandy dirt shoulder.

Cal tried to straighten up but could not. The front of his white shirt was quickly becoming totally crimson. He tried to smile at Cecilia, but it was hard since he was hemorrhaging from the mouth.

"Without me…to look after you, Ceci…you better stop burning so much rock –"

Tears ran down her face. "No, Cal. You can't leave me now. Don't go. Don't leave me! Cal!"

Cal had always thought it would be fun to die. He had looked forward to it, in a perverse, non-comprehending kind of way. He had killed many and, though most of his victims certainly did not seem to necessarily enjoy it, a few seemed to get off on it in an almost involuntarily sexual fashion. He longed for that supreme, galaxy-smashing orgasmic release he'd seen in the eyes and in the spontaneous shudders of some of his kills. But it was not happening for him. There was an excruciating dull ache pulsing around the perimeter of his bullet wounds and a slow, steady ebb of energy. It was tiring to die, slowly, and with only a teenage crackhead to mourn him.

Thinking of Ceci, he wondered for the first time just what it was inside of her that touched him, that made him care about her welfare when he had willfully, maliciously and often joyfully destroyed the welfare of so many others. She made him think of when he was an altar boy so many years before, and he had gotten drunk on the communion wine before serving, puking all over the paten, the pederast priest's hands and the face of the local mayor kneeling at the communion rail. The priest was the first one he'd killed, poison in a shrimp cocktail and no one had ever guessed. From there, each one had been easier. Why did he connect

Ceci up with that? Was there something about the way she sucked so greedily on the pipe, then sucked him off that reminded him of the priest? No. That couldn't be. More likely he related to Ceci's inexorably wistful desire for oblivion, her longing for death. That's what he suddenly felt with her there sitting beside him, clutching his shoulders spasmodically, trying to shake him awake and keep him from breathing his last.

Cal gave her one last smile and slumped towards her over the gear shift. She pulled both of her arms ever tighter around his expired form, obsessively embracing him.

Outside, in the serene midnight blue desert night, all that could be heard were the sounds of cicadas and of Cecilia weeping.

16

Someone was pounding on the narrow metal door beside the Warehouse's garage gate. Marilyn opened it to reveal Cecilia, dazed and the front of her covered with Cal's blood.

Marilyn peered over Ceci's shoulder to see the idling Buick, both doors open and headlights on. She was frightened, in spite of herself.

"Ceci, what happened? Where's Cal?" Marilyn shook her. "Where is Cal, Ceci?"

Ceci tried to respond, but the words would not come. Marilyn rushed past her to the passenger side of the car. She stopped as she caught sight of Cal's body.

Upstairs, Vanessa was still lying listlessly on the sofa. Cecilia appeared in the doorway and drifted slowly towards her. Vanessa was high as hell but not too high to register that something was seriously wrong with her friend. She struggled to a sitting position. Cecilia slowly sat down on the edge of the sofa, staring into space.

"Ceci, what's wrong, baby? Are you hurt?"

The traumatized girl could not answer.

Vanessa reached out to touch her. "Answer me, Ceci. What happened? Are you hurt?

Cecilia slowly turned to look at her, and shook her head, "Cal's dead. Your cousin Frankie killed him."

She pulled the .38 revolver that Cal had stolen from Frankie from her waistband and dreamily handed it to Vanessa. Vanessa's eyes widened. She looked over Cecilia's shoulder to make sure that Marilyn wasn't watching them, then took it, hiding it beneath the sofa cushions.

Four hours well after sundown, her headlights off, Frankie stopped her car at the bottom of the Richman house driveway. She quietly climbed out while making sure the interior light was covered. Stealthily she made her way up the inclined pavement.

All the lights were out in the living room except one lone soft spot over the plush sofa. Sexy slow jazz played low on the stereo. Marilyn was lying there, languidly stretched out in a black lace top and tight black leather pants. She sipped a bourbon on the rocks while perusing an ultra slick, sick S&M magazine. She smiled wickedly at something she was reading and took a sip of her drink. Almost imperceptibly the gun muzzle of Frankie's newly-acquired Glock appeared from behind Marilyn next to her right temple.

Marilyn still smiled, but her eyes darted to her right as Frankie's face appeared out of the darkness near the barrel nestling her ear.

"Hey, Frankie." Marilyn's greeting was deceptively cheerful. "I knew you'd be showing up sooner or later. After I had to deal with what was left of Cal."

"Dead, I hope."

"As a goddamn doornail. Tell me, did he do Jimmy before you got him? I couldn't get anything out of Ceci about what happened."

"Where is Jack, Marilyn?"

Marilyn was obnoxiously matter-of-fact. "Not anywhere in the vicinity. He took a new batch of girls into Vegas. You know he'll kill you for all this aggravation."

"The only one I care about right now is Vanessa. To be honest, I don't really care if I come out of this alive or not. But I'm going to make sure you two go down whatever-the-hell happens."

"The self-righteous martyr, as always."

"Spare me your appraisal of my character, Marilyn. I can see what you've been reading." She screwed the gun barrel deeper into Marilyn's ear.

"Where the fuck is Vanessa?"

"We've got her at the Warehouse. Grooming her for a higher purpose."

Frankie, still keeping the Glock to Marilyn's head, stepped over the sofa and yanked her to her feet.

"You fucking bitch. We're going to go get her. Right now."

The Mustang pulled up alongside the Warehouse entrance. Frankie was crouched low in the backseat, covering Marilyn with the Glock while Marilyn sat staring straight ahead.

"Just get him to open up. Like you do all the time. Nothing out of the ordinary. And remember, this is pointed right at the base of your spine."

Marilyn got out and banged petulantly on the corrugated metal door.

Marcus, their security man, saw Marilyn on the TV monitor, and he headed down to let her in. There was the sound of the door opening, and Frankie jumped out to stand directly behind the dominatrix.

Marcus groaned, "Ah, Jesus."

Frankie pushed Marilyn ahead of her through the entrance.

Marcus was mortified. "I'm sorry, Marilyn."

"Don't worry your pretty little head. Our guest will be taken care of soon enough."

Frankie gestured with the gun, "Stop your commiserating. Turn around, muscle boy, and lead us to Vanessa."

Right then Cecilia emerged from the bathroom below the stairway and caught sight of Frankie. She abruptly snapped out of her shell-shocked stupor and lunged at her nemesis.

"Goddamn you, you fucking bitch!"

Marilyn used the distraction to bolt up the stairs. Frankie tried to disentangle herself from Cecilia's clawlike grasp just as Marcus whirled, drawing his gun. She managed to kick Cecilia away from her as he fired and wounded her in the left hand.

Wincing with pain, Frankie strode boldly up to him, firing nearly point blank into his chest. The muscled Marcus died instantly, a look of shock and dismay on his squirrelly features.

Frankie glanced up the stairs, then quickly over to Cecilia on the floor. Keeping her eyes on Cecilia, she grabbed Marcus' 9 mm with her bleeding left hand and pocketed it.

Marilyn called from upstairs, "Hey, Frankie, where-the-hell are you? I thought you were in such a big hurry to see your little cousin, Vanessa."

Cecilia leapt to her feet and catapulted out the door into the dark wilderness.

Frankie moved cautiously up to the second story,

then inched through the door.

Immediately, there was the snap of Marilyn's bull-whip, and Frankie's gun went flying across the room.
Lit by a glowing amber light, it was a macabre, almost gothic scene. Black-clad Marilyn was poised behind the couch with the bullwhip looped in a stranglehold around Vanessa's throat. The lavender wall behind them made it look like an elaborate photo shoot for one of Marilyn's slick pervert magazines.

Marilyn softly laughed. "I can break her neck with a quick twist, Frankie. I've done it to little girls with big mouths before. Girls with a lot more fight in them than this strung-out bitch."

Vanessa was subtly, almost imperceptibly reaching down into the cushions of the couch.

Frankie was stoic, calmly letting her hand bleed on the floor.

Marilyn gloated, "Checkmate." Her gaze riveted on Frankie, Marilyn didn't see that Vanessa had drawn the .38 from the between the cushions. She brought it up to point directly beneath Marilyn's chin, and Marilyn was too shocked to react. Frankie drew Marcus' gun from her pocket, walked briskly forward and shot Marilyn in the heart.

Marilyn had a stunned, incredulous expression on her face as she stared down at her gushing-blood chest then up at Frankie before falling backwards to the floor. Vanessa leveled the gun at Frankie.

"I knew I couldn't trust Marilyn, Frankie. And I know you're nothing like her. But I'm so fucking turned around, I still don't know if I can really trust you either."

Frankie didn't say anything, just looked at her sadly. Slowly, deliberately she moved forward and gently pried the revolver from Vanessa's grasp. As Frankie sat down beside her, Vanessa collapsed into her arms, sobbing uncontrollably. Frankie soothingly caressed the back of her head.

"Come on, baby, we're going to get the hell out of here. I know some place where we'll both be safe. At least for a day or two."

Vanessa suddenly noticed Frankie's bleeding hand. She quickly tore the sleeve off her own blouse and wrapped Frankie's palm in the makeshift bandage. Frankie was touched as well as taken aback by Vanessa's abrupt show of concern.

Vanessa nodded at Marilyn's corpse. "I know where we can put her and Marcus. There's an industrial walk-in freezer downstairs."

17

It was a beautiful, rosy dawn when Frankie drove the Mustang slowly up the winding mountain road. Vanessa sat back in the bucket seat, leaning her disheveled mane of hair against the open window.

"I don't suppose you know where your dad is. Marilyn said he'd gone to Vegas."

"As far as I know, she was telling the truth. They'd gotten a new bunch of girls in early last night. He usually keeps them there for a week or two, getting them strung out on junk before he takes them into Nevada to his dealer. But he was nervous about everything that's been happening. He didn't want them to be there even overnight."

"Speaking of junk, how are you feeling? How long have they been pumping that shit into you?"

"I'm not sure. Pretty continuously every couple of hours since the night Valerie was killed."

"I don"t know if that's enough time to get you super strung-out. But you're probably going to start feeling fairly bad anytime now. Hopefully it won't last more than a couple of days."

At last, the Mustang pulled up alongside the little house nestled in a clearing off the high deep ravine of the mountain.

"This belongs to my dad...I haven't been up here since way before Rick and Joey died." Frankie swung open her door, but Vanessa reached out to catch her arm.

"You know he's going to find us. It's a fucking control issue with him. Especially after you killed Marilyn and the others. And then took me. His ego won't let –"

"I know. He won't stop till one of us – or all of us – is dead."

"I just don't want it to be you."

Frankie smiled at her, patted her hand and got out.

It was late afternoon, and they were sunning themselves on a large, high flat rock. Frankie sat cross-legged in blue jeans, bra and sunglasses. Vanessa, clad in panties, tank-top and sunglasses, lay flat on the stone surface. Frankie perched her shades atop her head, then surveyed the mountain road and surrounding rocky area through binoculars.

Valerie sniffled. "I think I feel a little better after throwing up so much."

Frankie was preoccupied. "Hhmmm..."

"So, what do you think happened since we left? Are you in any trouble with your job?"

Frankie put down the binoculars, laughing ruefully. She replaced her shades over her eyes and cocked her head to look at Vanessa.

"Probably. Cal shot Jimmy Chavez with my gun, then managed to get away with Ceci before he died. I'm sure our illustrious mayor Axelrod and my fellow deputy Knox will support whatever scenario your dad, Jack, cooks up for them. Manny Torres is an honest sheriff but he's no match for those three ganging up on him. Not to mention what went down at The Warehouse. Then, to top it off, us disappearing on them."

"You know, I forgot to mention it at the time, but I'm sure the surveillance video of the downstairs entrance recorded you killing Marcus. I know it was self-defense. If it's like you say, though, I'm sure they could twist it however they wanted. If I'd thought of it, I would have grabbed the tape when we split."

"Don't sweat it now. I just want to worry about what's right in front of us. Make sure we're ready for Jack."

They rested in silence for a few minutes. Frankie looked at the road with the binoculars one more time, then stretched out horizontally next to Vanessa.

"Have you thought of what you're going to do once Jack is finally out of the picture?"

"I'm not sure. I've got an aunt on my real mother's side in San Francisco. I could probably go live with her for a while."

"If they don't throw me in stir after all this, you know you could come to live with me."

Vanessa reached out to take hold of her hand.

After dark, the sky was an intoxicating indigo blue, and there was the nocturnal sound of insects and wildlife in the cooling summer air.

Frankie stood leaning against the sink behind the counter that separated the small kitchenette from the rest of the cabin. She poured herself a drink from a newly opened fifth of vodka. Vanessa was lying on the high double bed with the wrought iron headboard, and she tossed fitfully. Abruptly, she underwent a violent fit of retching into the pot by the bed. Frankie paused over her drink, first studying it and then watching Vanessa. The emotion welled up in her face. First, she poured the glass out, then the entire bottle of liquor, down the drain.

Later Frankie crawled up behind Vanessa and lay next to her in a spooning position, soothingly caressing Vanessa's perspiring forehead with a cold washrag. Residual alcohol sweated out of Frankie's pores, and the hours snaked by until she found herself sitting up against the headboard in candlelight, Vanessa sound asleep in the crook of her arm. She checked the ammunition clip of the Glock automatic.

At dawn, Frankie sat there alone, passed out against the headboard. Vanessa was nowhere in sight.

Vanessa bathed her face in the mountain stream, then sat back on her haunches, watching ravens circle in the sky. A small twitch of movement caught her eye, and she spotted a desert rat scurry along the bank carrying a large grasshopper in its mouth. She scooped up more water and threw it over her face, letting it run down her blouse and soak her breasts. She felt revived, suddenly charged with energy and began to pick her way amongst the stones as she climbed back towards the cabin. As she rose up over the last few rocks, what she saw made her stop cold in her tracks. Just beyond the Mustang, making his way towards the house with his back turned was her father, Jack Richman. He held a mean-looking .45 automatic clutched between both hands. Vanessa prayed Frankie had woken up. She could barely keep from angrily shouting warning, but she was afraid it would do more harm than good, so she just stared after Jack as he stealthily entered through the open cabin door. As soon as he was inside, she ran quietly to the Mustang, reached in the open passenger window to the glove compartment, pulled out Frankie's .38, then quickly headed to the cabin.

When Jack's shadow fell across Frankie's eyes, they sprang open. She aimed the Glock and pulled the trigger, but nothing happened. Jack had his .45 aimed straight at her, and he found her malfunctioning gun uproariously funny.

Jack tried his best to stop laughing, "That's kind of the story of your life, hunh, Frankie?"

Frankie let her gun arm fall to her side. "Jack, I cannot believe what you did to your own flesh and blood."

Jack found the comment annoying. "We're animals, Frankie. I take pride in not pretending to be anything else. When little wolf cubs can't cut it, they get cut loose by their parents. Or eaten alive."

"Fuck you."

"You never did. You don't know what you've missed."

"You sick fuck. You and Marilyn deserved each other. A match made in Hell."

"I love my wife."

"That's sweet. Still talking in the present tense. You haven't looked in the Warehouse freezer."

"What?"

"You'll see."

"If you've –"

"If I have what, Jack? Killed her? Like you did Rick?"

Jack's face was beet red. His grin widened with malice. "That's right. But you never knew all the details, did you?"

Frankie's face grew pale.

"I think I'll tell you. Yeah, I think I'll do that little thing. It's sunrise, but you're not going to live to see it set. So, this'll be like a little bedtime story, before I tuck you in for that long, long night's dirt nap."

"Go right ahead."

"You remember that weekend of the fire? Of course you do. Those days before it went down, you know Rick was in Vegas with me? He didn't tell you that, did he? Of course, you were three sheets to the wind as usual. Really, for all your concern about daughters – *my* daughters – you'd think you would have cared a bit more about the impression you were making on your son, Joey."

Frankie's complexion went whiter.

"We were doing a little movie shoot. Rick was looking forwards to it. All that delicious female flesh, exposed, squirming about. But there were a lot of things that Rick didn't count on happening. You do things like that, having a wild time, going as far out as you can, sometimes people go too far. There were some bondage scenes, and Rick fancied one of the women –"

"I don't believe you."

"It doesn't matter whether you believe me or not. This girl, she was the exact opposite of you, Frankie. Not a blonde bone in her body. High yellow they used to call them. Black hair, green eyes. She liked it plenty rough. Marilyn pulled her. Anyway, things got out of hand. Rick was there, hanging around on the set. He'd had plenty to drink. He saw what happened. Yolonda was her name. Unfortunately, she got her neck broken. At first, Rick wanted us to report it. I convinced him it wouldn't be a good idea. He finally came around to the wisdom of that position. He was upset, but things would've worked out fine if he hadn't overheard Marilyn talking…" His voice trailed off, and he smiled.

"And?"

"Are you sure you want to know, Frankie? It isn't pretty, and it isn't nice."

"Fuck off. Tell your goddamn story and get it over with."

"Marilyn was into very rough stuff from the time

she reached puberty. She had bad influences from her family and friends. But she never shrank away from it, and she embraced it from the beginning, unlike Val and Van, who always put up a struggle. She knew Cal from the time she was in high school. He was in 8th grade and she was in 12th when they met. They used to get together for torture sessions with cats and dogs."

"You make me sick."

"They used to procure teenage boys for a sex ring in Dallas."

"Get to the goddamn punchline."

"Rick heard Marilyn talking to Cal."

"About?"

"About how cute Joey was and wouldn't it be awful nice if they could get him in a cameo for their next film. Cal agreed. Marilyn started suggesting various scenarios…"

Frankie was silently, subtly working the Glock, trying to massage it into a more helpful state. Her face had gone from white to red, flaming with a fiery anger she tried to contain so she wouldn't end up getting herself shot any sooner than Jack had planned.

Jack could see the effect he was having on his niece, and he was happy to rub it in, especially after Frankie had been vindictive and had gone to the trouble of implying Marilyn was dead.

"Cal and Marilyn had both been smoking meth and drinking bourbon. They were cranked up. Cal said he was sure he could make some special arrangements. The two dumbbells didn't know Rick was right on the other side of the door. Finally, he exploded and coldcocked Cal and slapped Marilyn silly. I tried to settle him down, telling him not to pay attention to them, the speed and alcohol had them too hopped up. But he wouldn't listen. He said he wasn't going to keep quiet about Yolonda biting the dust in

our little S&M movie. All bets were off. He was going to
report it to Vegas PD and tell Manny on Monday morning,
if not sooner. Rick had been drinking, too, and he spilled
all kinds of things about Bakersfield and Fresno and
Victorville coordinating with Palm Springs and across
state lines with Vegas PD, how there were already Feds
crawling around, looking into sex slave rings and interstate
prostitution. He brought up all the shit Marilyn and I got
him to do to help me with Clancy Hepburn's murder."

"What shit?"

"Oh, I guess he never mentioned it to you. He
must've been embarassed, the wuss. He faked evidence that
cleared me. He believed me when I told him I had nothing
to do with it. I'd say he was a gullible cocksucker, but I
think he knew deep in his heart of hearts that I was guilty.
You know what I think it was? He was worried about you.
Your dad, Nick, the son-of-a-bitch, knew I'd done it, . He
couldn't prove anything though. I killed Clancy when he
backtracked on the Salamanca Estates deal. The prick."

Jack let it sink in. Frankie's face was ashen.

"Anyway, Rick kept shouting at us till he was
hoarse. Marilyn and Cal wanted to do him right there, but
I wanted to wait till he was back in Sweet Home, hoping
against hope he'd come to his senses. But I think in *my*
very own heart of hearts, I knew better. It was too bad Joey
was there. We'd had word he was still at Nick's, since you
were always on night shift. But he got home early."

Vanessa padded noiselessly up behind her father and
leveled the .38 against the nape of his neck. He was visibly
shocked that Vanessa had trumped his hand.

"Daddy, you are so full of shit."

Frankie watched, powerless, from the bed.

"I feel weird about calling you daddy. You're not
the dad type. You're the Jack Richman type. So I'll call you
what you always used to like me and Val to call you. Jack.

Put that gun down on the bed next to Frankie, Jack."

Jack did not move.

"You better do it, you son-of-a-bitch. Don't give me the satisfaction. After what you've done to Val, what you've done to me, to my mother, I'm just biding my time till I see you six feet under."

He reluctantly complied with her order, then turned ever so slowly to face her.

"Jack, I've always wanted to know, and every time I ask you, you never, ever will tell me. Why did you commit mom to the asylum?"

For some reason, of all things, this topic made him uncomfortable. "What're you talking about?"

"You know. Why did you do it?"

"All right. You want to know? I got sick of her trying to rein me in. I got sick of her being grossed out every time I wanted to fuck her. I got sick of her writing her goddamn poetry in the middle of the goddamn fucking night."

"Marilyn pushed you?"

"She just gave me the guts to do it. Meeting Marilyn was the best thing that ever happened to me. She showed me how to go all the way in every area of my business and my personal life. No fucking limits, no fucking regrets."

Vanessa was very calm. "You ruined mom's life. You fucked up all those young girls. You fucked me up and killed Val. And now you've done your best to destroy Frankie."

Jack laughed, "Frankie? Frankie's pretty much destroyed herself. " He turned towards his niece. "You always thought you were so tough, Frankie. I was tickled pink when I got to burn up your self-righteous son-of-a-bitch, no good pig husband."

Frankie's jaw set, and her eyes narrowed almost imperceptibly.

Jack turned back to Vanessa, a hideous smile on his face. "But you want to know what really made me happiest, Van? You want to know? When I got to choke the living daylights out of your two-timing sister. Her running off and replacing me with that scum Jimmy Chavez. Her having the gall to say to me, 'No, daddy, I'm not going to fuck you anymore.'"

Before he could even say another word, Vanessa fired the .38 three times, emptying the rest of the bullets into Jack's chest. Jack grabbed his gushing blood front and slumped back on the bed next to Frankie. He smiled at her. She stared at him coldly as he breathed his last wheezing breath.

Frankie slowly turned to Vanessa, and they locked stares.

18

Frankie was still unconscious in the hospital bed. Her pupils convulsed in r.e.m. beneath her bruised eyelids. Somewhere in the ether, blue flames reared up around her, turning bright orange, then yellow, then finally a blinding white light, destroying her happy suburban home so many years before.

Vanessa and Manny Torres stared down at her comatose body.

"You know she didn't kill Jimmy Chavez. Cal Nero did. You know she didn't kill my dad. I killed the son-of-a-bitch."

Torres was out of his depth, "Vanessa, we got her a good attorney. But Axelrod's prosecution had too much circumstantial evidence. Chavez and Jack were both killed with her gun." He lost it. "This town, goddamn it, it's still Jack Richman's town. He's dead, but it's still his town. No matter what we do."

Nick Powers rolled into the room in his wheelchair.

"Don't worry about it now, Manny. You did your best. Frankie did her best, too. Even though none of those mooks on the jury saw it that way. It's too goddamn fucking late now."

Suddenly the heart monitor began loudly humming, giving way to a high-pitched squeal. Two nurses and a doctor rushed into the room as Frankie flatlined.

"All of you will have to leave."

Vanessa, Torres and Nick followed their directions and clustered just outside the room. Their attention to the doctor's efforts to save Frankie was rapt and intense. Vanessa was doing her best not to cry.

Frankie was gone.

The doctor called the time of death. Frankie's face seemed to relax, and assumed a serene calm that was hauntingly beautiful.

Vanessa swung around resolutely from the others and walked away from them down the hall. Torres and Nick both turned to look after her.

Nick called out, "Vanessa!"

It was late afternoon outside the hospital as Vanessa strode purposefully down the sidewalk and up the street. After five minutes walk, she came to the bus station. Her chin propped on one hand, she sat down to forlornly wait on the outside bench.

A half hour later, she climbed onto the Greyhound, and a few minutes after that it pulled onto the highway. She wasn't even sure exactly where it was going. But she had some money Frankie had given her, probably enough to get her to San Francisco, she thought. She pressed her face against the window, watching the twilight squalor of Sweet Home give way to the desert wilderness.

Chris D. is also author of the novels *NO EVIL STAR, MOTHER'S WORRY, SHALLOW WATER* and the collection *DRAGON WHEEL SPLENDOR AND OTHER LOVE STORIES OF VIOLENCE AND DREAD*, all from Poison Fang Books. His anthology *A MINUTE TO PRAY, A SECOND TO DIE*, a 500 page collection of selected short stories, excerpts from novels and scores of dream journal entries, as well as all of his poetry and song lyrics, was published in December 2009. His non-fiction *OUTLAW MASTERS OF JAPANESE FILM* was published by IB Tauris (distributed by Palgrave Macmillan in the USA) in 2005. He saw release of his first feature film as director, *I PASS FOR HUMAN*, in 2004 (and its DVD release in 2006), and worked as a programmer at The American Cinematheque in Hollywood, California from 1999-2009. Chris D. is also known as the singer/songwriter of the bands The Flesh Eaters, Divine Horsemen and Stone by Stone. He was an A&R rep and in-house producer at Slash Records/Ruby Records from 1980-1984. April 2013 saw the release of his 800 page non-fiction *GUN AND SWORD: AN ENCYCLOPEDIA OF JAPANESE GANGSTER FILMS 1955-1980*. His latest are the novels *VOLCANO GIRLS* and *TIGHTROPE ON FIRE*, from Poison Fang Books. Upcoming works include the novel, *TATTOOED BLOOD.*.

Thank yous to Donna Lethal, Sylvie Simmons, Alan K. Rode, Byron Coley, Lili Dwight, Craig Owens, Wayne Valdez of Store 54, Peter Maravelis of City Lights, Gwen Deglise, Craig Clevenger, Eddie Muller, Taquila Mockingbird, Shepherd Stevenson, Richard Lange, Liz Garo & Alex Maslansky & Claudia Colodro of Stories, Billy Shire & Matt Kennedy of Wacko/La Luz de Jesus, Dan Kusunoki of Skylight Books, Curtis Tsui, Joey O'Brien, Liz Helfgott, John Roller, Tosh Berman of Tam Tam Books, Feeding Tube Records in Northampton, Other Music in Manhattan

NO EVIL STAR

a novel by CHRIS D.

The life of recovering addict and Namvet Milo unravels when ex-CIA friend Dave goes off the deep end. Not only is Dave the heist man whacking NYC drug dealers, he's also hatching a scheme to plunder mob boss Nunzio's art treasures pilfered in WWII. Complicating matters, Yuen, an ex-Viet Cong with a grudge against Milo and Dave, arrives in New York.

"A healthy authorial sense of curiosity and generosity lends weight to No Evil Star's intersecting lives, where Chris D. ably traces out the contours of human torment in a manner recalling American films of the 1970s."
– Grace Krilanovich, author of The Orange Eats Creeps

AVAILABLE NOW FROM POISON FANG BOOKS

In Chris D.'s title novella, brilliant, alcoholic Anne, unable to succeed in downtown L.A.'s arts community, helps a Japanese-American girl escape forced prostitution, only to ignite a string of violent deaths. In "The Glider," a British policewoman falls in-love with a serial killer near the white cliffs of Dover; plus five more twisted love tales.

"...seems to shimmer with menace... with Dragon Wheel Splendor, the great Chris D should finally find the audience he deserves...a book that can kill the voices in your head - or make you love them."
– Jerry Stahl, author of Plainclothes Naked, Painkillers and Permanent Midnight

DRAGON WHEEL SPLENDOR
and Other Love Stories of Violence and Dread
by Chris D.

"...shimmers with menace...the great Chris D. should finally find the audience he deserves..."
– Jerry Stahl

The year is 1987, and outlaw Ray Diamond's mother is the queenpin of crime in Mystic, GA. After his Navy discharge, Ray knocks over a mob-connected El Paso liquor store, not counting on Eli, the owner's psycho son, dogging his trail. Back home in Mystic, Ray's girl, Connie Eustace, resorts to stripping at Mama Lorna's club to make ends meet. Witness to a murder by the local sheriff, she goes on a drug-and-drink bender, jumping from the frying pain into the fire.

MOTHER'S WORRY

a novel
by
CHRIS D.

"...a crazy dive into a universe populated largely by monsters...a classic update of the Gold Medal/Lion Library loser noir tradition. Great work... "
– Byron Coley, writer for WIRE magazine, author of C'EST LA GUERRE: EARLY WRITINGS 1978-1983

SHALLOW WATER

A Southern Gothic Noir Western
by
CHRIS D.

Post-Civil War, bitter rebel veteran and bounty hunter, Santo Brady, drifts through the Deep South. When he rescues halfbreed Indian prostitute, Lucy Damien, from one backwater town, he has the world fall in on his head. They embark on a freight-train-hopping odyssey to New Orleans, unaware that Lucy's rich white father and homicidal brother are tracking them. A tragic tall tale plunging head-first into a wild heart of darkness.

"One sinsister serpent of a story, an old Republic Pictures western serial scripted by James M. Cain and reimagined by Sam Peckinpah. I loved it."
– Eddie Muller, author of THE DISTANCE and SHADOW BOXER

Two New Novels from Chris D.
Available October 2013

Half-sisters, schoolteacher Mona and junkie punk rocker Terri, are uneasy roommates while taking care of their sick mother. When their boyfriends, cop Johnny Cullen and killer Merle Chambers, clash due to labor struggles in their small town of Devil's River, the two women are pulled into the fray. To make matters worse, jealous female sheriff, Billie Travers, decides Mona is intruding on her faltering love affair, and quiet small town life amps up into an apocalyptic nightmare of uncontrollable violence and destruction.

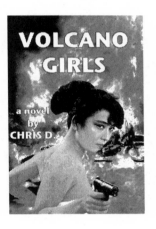

Corrupt female police detective, Frankie Powers, is treading water in her small desert hometown of Sweet Home, California. Burned-out and emotionally numb after losing her husband and child in a mysterious fire ten years before, her conscience is reawakened when her affair with a Bakersfield narc brings new facts to light. Frankie's mob boss uncle, Jack Richman, has been kidnapping under-age girls for his Vegas prostitution syndicate; he's also been victimizing his own teen daughters, Frankie's twin bad girl cousins, Valerie and Vanessa. Soon Frankie finds herself singlehand-edly fighting tooth-and-nail against not only wicked uncle Jack but also his dominatrix wife, Marilyn and their degenerate hitman, Cal Nero. Can a lone shewolf survive against the bloodthirsty pack?

from **P**oison **F**ang **B**ooks

Made in the USA
Columbia, SC
09 November 2022

70684079R00069